LUCKY 13

Look for these and other books in the *Teen Witch* series:

Lucky 13
Be Careful What You Wish For
Gone with the Witch
Witch Switch

LUCKY 13

MEGAN BARNES

SCHOLASTIC INC.
New York Toronto London Auckland Sydney

ISBN 0-590-41296-5

12 11 10 9 8 7 6 5 4 3 2   8 9/8 0 1 2 3/9

Printed in the U.S.A.   01

First Scholastic printing, October 1988

Chapter 1

Sarah Connell opened one sleep-fogged eye and tried to focus on the shadowy form that loomed menacingly over her bed. It was her fifteen-year-old sister, Nicole — that much was obvious. But why was Nicole yelling and waving her arms around? Sarah wondered hazily. She tried to pull the covers over her long brown hair and drift back into a wonderful dream about Kirk Tanner, but her sister was too fast for her.

Nicole pounced like a rabbit and swept Sarah's patchwork quilt onto the floor. Sarah loved country prints, and her room was splashed with bright chintz curtains and braided rugs.

"Don't even *think* of going back to sleep, Sarah!" Nicole yelled. "I'm not going to leave this room without my Tangerine Ice lip gloss, so you may as well confess right this minute."

"What are you talking about?" Sarah croaked, sitting up and blinking dazedly. Her brown eyes looked puzzled, and she shivered, tucking her long slim legs under her.

"My lip gloss," Nicole repeated icily. Her sleek blonde pageboy quivered as she spat out the words. "I know you took it, and I want it back. Now! Although how you'll ever find it in this mess is beyond me." She walked to the window and gave the drapery cord a vicious yank. Daylight flooded the bedroom, and Sarah winced. It felt as if someone were shredding her eyeballs.

"Nicole," Sarah said, swinging her legs over the side of the bed, "I do not have . . . nor have I ever had . . . the alleged item in my possession." She liked that speech, she decided, stumbling to the mirror. She had heard it the night before on an old *Perry Mason* episode and had memorized it on the spot. You never knew when a phrase like that would come in handy. That day was the perfect example.

"Then if you don't have it, *where* is it?" Nicole said, her pale blue eyes narrowing. Nicole was usually the most controlled person in the world, but when she was upset, her voice rose to an unpleasant shriek. Right now, Sarah thought, she sounded like a blender with sinus problems.

Sarah started to pull a brush through her tangled dark hair, then stopped. "Nicole," she said reasonably, "think about it. Do I look like someone who would wear Tangerine Ice lip gloss?" She pointed to the corkboard that took up part of one wall. It was festooned with dozens of clothing ads torn out of fashion magazines. Sarah's dream was to be a designer, and the board served as an inspiration for her own sketches. "If you bothered to study *Seventeen*, you'd know that citrus colors are *out*, and hot pinks are *in*. You should throw out your old lip gloss and buy some of the new bubble-gum shades."

"Thanks so much for the advice," Nicole said through gritted teeth. "Now, I'm going to give you exactly ten seconds to come up with that lip gloss." She took a step forward, banging her knee on an open dresser drawer. "Ten!" she yelled. "Nine, eight, seven, six. . . ."

"Take it easy!" Sarah muttered, staring at herself in the mirror. She really should get a new nightshirt, she thought idly. Her "Morris" shirt was so old that the famous cat face was missing its whiskers and ears, giving Morris a rodentlike look. Just the other day, her best friend, Micki, had asked her why she was wearing a shirt with a guinea pig on the front.

"Three . . . two. . . ." Nicole's face was a thundercloud, and she looked ready to explode. Sarah couldn't help wondering if steam would pour out of her ears, like it did on the Saturday morning cartoon shows.

"One!" Nicole waited, red with anger, while Sarah turned slowly from the mirror.

"I *don't* have it — " Sarah began, but her sister was already stomping furiously toward the door.

"You'll pay for this, Sarah," she hissed. "You just wait and see!"

After Nicole ran out of the room, Sarah shrugged and stared at herself in the mirror. Nothing like a fight with your sister to get the adrenaline flowing, she thought wryly. She was definitely awake now, she decided, noticing the red flush creeping into her cheeks. She gave a catlike stretch and glanced at the clock. Seven-thirty already! She'd be late for breakfast, and worst of all, Micki was coming by to pick her up that morning.

Sarah showered quickly and pulled on a pair of jeans and a gold metallic blouse she had found in a flea market. She would have liked to have worn her sleek new Italian boots, but there was no time to hunt for them in the back of her closet. Besides, she could hear a familiar giggle drifting in from the kitchen. Micki Davis was waiting for her.

"I can't believe you eat this way every day," Micki was saying, when Sarah rushed into the kitchen a few minutes later. Micki was sitting at the breakfast table, staring at a heaping platter of pancakes topped with yogurt and blueberries. "I feel like I just wandered onto the set of *Who's the Boss?*" Micki's yellow shetland sweater set off her bright red hair and creamy complexion. She was a little shorter than Sarah and preferred pleated wool skirts to jeans.

"That's what happens when your father is a doctor," Sarah said, sliding into the seat next to Micki. "He insists that breakfast is the most important meal of the day." She speared a pancake and said worriedly, "Do I have time to eat something?"

"Only if you inhale it," Micki teased her. "We've got to be at school in twenty minutes." She turned to Mrs. Connell, who was pouring her a glass of orange juice. "Where is Dr. Connell this morning?"

"Oh, he started office hours a little early today," Sarah's mother explained. "It's the flu season, you know. I brought him some coffee a few minutes ago, and the office is already filling up." David Connell was a busy pediatrician, who kept a suite of offices in a separate wing of the house.

"I'm sorry to keep you waiting," Sarah said to Micki between mouthfuls of pancake. "Have you been here long?"

Micki nodded and laughed. "Yeah, and I've enjoyed every minute of it. I'm so stuffed, I may even skip lunch." Her brown eyes sparkled with amusement.

"What happened, Sarah?" Mrs. Connell asked. "Did you oversleep?"

"Not exactly," Sarah said, smiling across the table at Nicole. "I was having this awful nightmare about someone breaking into my room and threatening me. It was terrible! They kept screaming at me and accusing me of something I didn't do." She shook her head slowly. "I was terrified."

"Hmm," Karen Connell said thoughtfully. "It sounds to me like you've been watching those horror movies on cable again. You know you always get nightmares from them." She flipped open the newspaper and took a quick look at the headlines, before slipping into her tailored blue blazer.

"Oh, Mom!" Nicole burst out disgustedly, "she's putting you on. She didn't have a nightmare. I was in her room this morning — to get back something that belongs to *me*."

"Really?" Sarah said in mock amazement. "That monster was you? I thought it had fangs."

"Very funny," Nicole sniffed.

"What are you missing, Nicole?" Mrs. Connell asked absently. She reached for a thick pile of manila folders and put a rubber band around them. Karen Connell was a tall, attractive woman with glossy black hair and dark eyes. She was a guidance counselor at a small private school, and frequently brought work home with her.

"My Tangerine Ice lip gloss," Nicole said eagerly. "Have you seen it?"

"No, I'm afraid I haven't," Mrs. Connell admitted. "But I'm sure it will turn up somewhere."

"What will turn up?" Simon Connell asked, sauntering into the kitchen. At seventeen, Simon's main interest in life was sports, and he was wearing a ragged football jersey with torn sleeves. He grabbed an apple and an orange out of the fruit bowl before sitting down.

"I'm missing my Tangerine Ice lip gloss,"

Nicole said to her brother, raising her eyes to the ceiling. "I don't suppose you know anything about it."

"*Moi?*" Simon said comically. "Of course not." He paused and pretended to think. Suddenly he snapped his fingers. "Wait a minute. I needed an orange Magic Marker for my poster last night — "

"Simon!"

"Relax, I'm just kidding." He reached for the pancakes just as Micki and Sarah stood up to leave. "Hey, why are you running off? Was it something I said?" He put on his Rodney Dangerfield voice, and Micki giggled appreciatively.

"We have to go, we'll be late for homeroom." Micki laughed again.

Nicole glanced at her watch and groaned. "I'll just have to go without lip gloss today. Not that anyone cares," she added dramatically.

"Oh, really, Nicole," Sarah said automatically. "Go look in the bottom of your closet. The lip gloss is right there, in your sneaker." As Nicole dashed from the room, Sarah said softly, "Did I really say that?"

"You sure did," Micki told her. "Now can we please go? We're going to end up with a pink slip."

"You're on!" Sarah said, heading for the door. They were in the front hall, when they heard Nicole give an earsplitting shriek. "I found the lip gloss. Right in my sneaker. I'm going to kill you for this, Sarah!"

Sarah and Micki stared at each other and shrugged. "Some people have no gratitude," Sarah said.

"I thought you didn't know anything about it," Micki pointed out.

"That's the funny thing," Sarah said, looking bewildered. "I didn't."

"Very strange," Micki muttered, as they stepped out into the bright October sunshine.

It sure is! Sarah agreed silently.

"You have to admit it was kind of spooky," Micki said eagerly at lunch that day. "After all, you said that you had no idea where the lip gloss was and I believed you, and then suddenly you knew it was in Nicole's sneaker."

They were sitting in the Waterview High School cafeteria, picking listlessly at their microwaved hamburgers. Both girls had nearly identical class schedules and ate lunch together every day.

Sarah shrugged. "I wouldn't call it spooky," she said. "Maybe a little odd, that's all."

"It was spooky," Micki repeated firmly. Her short red hair slid onto her cheeks, as she nodded her head vigorously.

"It was a coincidence," Sarah explained patiently. She peered at her hamburger and made a face. "I wonder why the microwave can't understand medium rare."

"At least it's consistent," Micki offered. "It cremates everything."

This brought a chuckle from Matt Neville, a brown-haired boy who was sitting across the table from them. Quiet and very bright, Matt was the kind of person who could make a solar converter out of a paper clip. Matt had been friends with Micki and Sarah since all three of them had been in play school together, and he usually joined them for lunch. He had been reading *The New York Times*, but now he pushed his glasses up on his forehead and peered at his two friends.

"According to the laws of probability, it's very unlikely that your knowledge of the lip gloss was a coincidence."

Sarah and Micki exchanged a look. Sometimes Matt sounded as if he had swallowed a physics book.

"Try that in English," Micki said with a sigh.

Matt put the paper aside and gave her an

earnest look. "Let's be rational about this," he began, and Sarah started to giggle. The whole problem with Matt was, he was *always* rational! She was sure he would grow up to be a scientist or maybe a college professor. He was dressed in his favorite outfit: neatly pressed khakis and a pastel shirt with a button-down collar. A little conservative for Sarah's tastes, but exactly right for Matt.

"I meant that random chance just doesn't explain it," Matt ventured. "I think on some level" — the glasses slipped back on his nose, giving him an owlish look — "Sarah *knew* the lip gloss was in the sneaker."

Sarah raised a skeptical eyebrow. "Oh, come on," she said. "Are you saying it's possible to know something without really knowing that you know it?"

"Absolutely." Matt laughed. "Of course this is all speculation. None of us can say for sure what happened."

The bell rang just then, and Sarah was thoughtful as she gathered up her books.

"It's amazing what you can do with spinach," Sarah's father said at dinner later that evening. Dr. David Connell was tall and blond, with crinkly blue eyes, and an ear-to-ear grin that put his patients at ease. Since his offices were in the Connell home, Sarah had grown up with the sound of wailing babies and eternally ringing phones.

"What do you call this?" Simon asked suspiciously. He poked his plate gingerly, as if he were afraid the soggy green mass might reach out and grab him.

"Vegetable lasagna," Mrs. Connell said brightly.

"But why is it — "

"It's green because it's made from spinach noodles." She smiled warmly. One of the dangerous things about having a mother who was a guidance counselor was that she always was one jump ahead of you, Sarah thought with amusement. Sometimes Sarah's friends accused her mother of reading their minds, but Sarah knew better. Karen Connell had been dealing with teenagers for so long that she just automatically tuned in to their thoughts and feelings.

"Great source of iron," Dr. Connell put in. He grew his own vegetables and was always pleased when they showed up on the family dinner table.

Sarah ate quickly, hiding most of her lasagna under a lettuce leaf, and was clearing the table when her mother approached her.

"I had a little talk with Nicole," Mrs. Connell began. "And . . . well, is there anything you want to tell me?"

"I didn't take her lip gloss," Sarah said flatly, and was rewarded with a startled look from her mother. "I don't know why she thinks I did."

Mrs. Connell shrugged. "Well, you have to admit, it sounds pretty bizarre. How could you possibly know the lip gloss was in her sneaker, unless you put it there?"

Sarah shook her head. "I can't explain it, Mom. You'll just have to take my word for it."

Her mother looked at her for a long moment. "You know, sometimes we take things we don't even want . . . or need," she said thoughtfully.

"Only if we're kleptomaniacs," Sarah retorted.

Mrs. Connell's lips started to twitch, and Sarah knew she was trying not to laugh. "All right," she said finally. "I'll let it go this time. If you say you didn't take it, I believe you. I suppose stranger things have happened."

"Wouldn't it be wonderful if there were a little pill you could take, and it had all the vitamins and calories and everything you needed for the whole day?" It was the following day and Tina Jordan was standing next to Sarah in the cafeteria lunch line. Tina was a stunning black girl, with a reed-thin figure and enormous brown eyes.

"I guess so," Sarah said dubiously. "It would kind of take all the fun out of eating, though."

"You call this fun?" Micki snorted. "Listen to what they've got today." She peered at the blackboard that hung over the serving counter. "Tuna Surprise . . . hah! I don't know what's so surprising about it. Every Thursday they stuff some tuna into a squishy old tomato. . . ."

"The only surprise would be if they put a Cracker Jack prize inside," Matt said. "And look, there's Meat Loaf Supreme."

"What's that like?" Micki asked.

"I don't know, but it's supremely awful," he joked, and everyone cracked up.

"We could try the special — it's something called Braised Beef," Sarah said, reaching for a tray. She jumped as Kirk Tanner put his hand over hers.

"Don't!" he pleaded. "It violates your Constitutional rights."

"It does?" Sarah gasped. She knew Kirk was teasing, and she tried not to notice that his hand was still touching hers. Tall and good-looking, with cool gray eyes and a terrific smile, Kirk was one of the most popular boys in school. Sarah had had a crush on him for as long as she could remember, but would have died rather than admit it to anyone but Micki.

"Definitely," he told her. "There's a provision against cruel and unusual punishment."

"Oh," she said, laughing nervously and withdrawing her hand. He was standing very close to her, and Sarah suddenly felt awkward and embarrassed. "You know what I think?" she blurted out. "I think we deserve something great for lunch today. Something like pizza!"

Suddenly, the loudspeaker crackled to life. A bored voice said: "Lunch will be delayed due to a breakdown in the stoves. Pizza is being ordered from Luigi's and will be here within ten minutes."

Micki turned to stare at Sarah, her jaw dropping open in surprise. "I can't believe it!" she said incredulously.

"Hey, way to go!" Kirk said, clapping his hands. "Pizza at Waterview High, this has got to be a first." He whipped out his notebook and headed for the kitchen. "This can be my lead editorial for the *Sentry*," he said, smiling over his shoulder at Sarah. Kirk was the editor of the school paper, and never missed a chance at a story.

Matt scratched his head thoughtfully and adjusted his glasses. "Maybe I should rethink what I said about coincidences," he teased. "You're averaging one a day."

"It looks that way," Sarah agreed happily.

Chapter 2

As soon as Sarah appeared in the doorway to the kitchen the next morning, her family all yelled together, "Happy birthday!"

"What do you think — is this a dynamite outfit, or what? Perfect for a girl entering her teens?" Sarah posed in the doorway, and her family looked at her in surprise.

Dr. Connell was the first to recover. "You look like you're on your way to an appendectomy, Sarah," he said, taking in the wrinkled green scrub suit cinched with a wide leather belt.

"Yeah, your own," Simon said, turning his attention back to his physics book. Mrs. Connell didn't like anyone to read at the table, but in Simon's case it was a necessity. A talented athlete and popular student, Simon never claimed to be a scholar. He scraped by most of his classes with low C's, occasionally hitting a B in subjects like band and phys ed.

"Yuck!" Nicole said feelingly. "You look like you dressed at a rummage sale."

Nicole looked cool and preppy this warm October morning, with her blonde hair sleeked back in a ponytail, and tiny pearl studs in her ears. She was dressed in a pink oxford cloth blouse and a pair of white cotton Izod pants. She peered at Sarah's wrinkled green scrub suit more closely. PROPERTY OF ST. FRANCIS HOSPITAL was stamped in large letters on the back of the shirt, and the drawstring pants were frayed at the edges. "You remind me of something," she said thoughtfully.

"An unmade bed?" Simon asked.

Sarah took a playful swipe at her brother before taking her place at the table. "I can't help it if none of you has any fashion sense," she said good-naturedly. She was used to her family making fun of her outrageous outfits. "If this had a Gucci label on it, it would cost hundreds of dollars."

"If that outfit had a Gucci label on it, Gucci would be out of business," Nicole hooted.

"I saved you some of that blackstrap molasses you love," Dr. Connell said, passing her a sticky jar of what looked like coal tar. "You might want to try some on the buckwheat pancakes I made this morning, especially for your thirteenth birthday."

"Do they have spinach in them?" Sarah kidded him.

He winked at her. "No, but they have a secret ingredient."

"Don't ask what it is," Simon muttered.

"Aunt Pam called this morning," her mother told her. "She said happy birthday and could you give her a hand in the bookstore after school today. She just received a new shipment of paperbacks and hasn't had a chance to unpack them."

"That's probably because she's trying to read them all at the same time." Sarah laughed.

Pamela Huntley, Sarah's aunt, was rarely without a book in her hand, and usually was reading several books at once. Her combination bookstore and tea shop, Plates and Pages, was a bustling, happy place filled with exotic scents and dozens of wind chimes that tinkled as you brushed past them. Sarah loved to spend hours there, helping with the inventory, and talking to her amazing aunt.

"Sure, I'll be glad to go," Sarah told her mother. "I'll be ready for a break after school today. I've got a French quiz, an English report, and an algebra test. What a way to spend a birthday."

Mrs. Connell shrugged sympathetically. "Not one of your better days, I'm afraid. But hitting thirteen, entering your teen years, is an occasion. We'll celebrate at dinner."

"It's going to be one of the worst days of my life!" Sarah proclaimed. "Maturity brings responsibility, I guess," she said seriously.

The morning started out in a very ordinary way. She and Micki and Matt decided to duck into the cafeteria before the early bell rang. They headed for the concession area and Sarah was about to pump change into the soft drink machine when she stopped suddenly.

"What's wrong?" Micki said, nearly colliding with her.

"I can't do it," Sarah said simply.

"You're on a health kick again?" Matt asked wearily. He reached past her and punched a button. "Come on, we're having a birthday toast."

"No, it's not that," she said, a little embarrassed. "It's just that I've got this oral report due in English today. . . ."

"And carbonated drinks make her hiccup!" Micki finished for her.

This was the moment when Sarah made the decision that would change her life. "I've got to have something else . . . maybe hot chocolate."

"Hot chocolate?" Micki giggled. "In Southern California — you've got to be kidding!"

"No, I'm sure I've seen it in one of the machines," Sarah insisted. "I think it's the one right inside the teacher's lounge."

Micki rolled her eyes. "Sarah, that's way at the other end of the building. Look, split a Coke with me. Just this once, you can hiccup your way through the Middle Ages."

Sarah shook her head and slung her knapsack over her shoulder. "No way! I'll catch up with you in English."

When Sarah reached the teacher's lounge a few minutes late, she was in for the surprise of her life. Not only did she find hot chocolate — she came across the best-looking boy she had ever seen!

He was tall, with dark hair and intense blue eyes that reminded her of the Pacific Ocean on a sunny day. He was frowning when she spotted him, but even that didn't detract from his terrific looks. It just made him more interesting-looking.

He was wearing a blue shirt that matched his eyes exactly, and Sarah watched spellbound as he fumbled in his pockets for change. She stood frozen to the spot, and suddenly he turned and looked at her.

"Do you happen to have change for a dollar?" he asked in a low voice.

Sarah tried to speak, gulped, and tried again. "Change for a dollar?" she rasped. She had hoped her voice would come out low and sultry, but to her horror she sounded like an eight-year-old with a head cold.

He nodded, and showed her a one-dollar bill. Like an idiot, Sarah leaned over and inspected it.

He laughed gently. "It's not counterfeit," he said, snapping it.

"I know that," she blurted out. "I mean . . . here . . ." She dumped her knapsack on the floor and rummaged in her scrub suit for change. She could hear coins jingling in the yards of green cotton. It was like trying to find a nickel in a parachute. Frantically, she turned the pockets inside out, her pulse racing.

"I can get change for you," she croaked. "I can go to the cafeteria — " The cafeteria! She would have gone to Mars to get change for this boy.

"Hey, thanks anyway. I found some," he said. He reached into his jacket pocket and held up four quarters triumphantly. "Here we go," he said, pumping quarters into the machine. Sarah watched speechlessly as he handed her a steaming cup of hot chocolate.

"You don't have to do that," she protested.

The boy just smiled and shook his head. "My treat."

Sarah was so nervous she took a gulp of the hot chocolate and nearly yelped. It felt like someone was pouring hot lava down her throat.

"I really get sick of soft drinks, you know?" the boy told her.

Sarah nodded solemnly as if he had just said something profound. She tried to look thoughtful, pretending to digest the information.

The bell rang just then, and the boy shifted his books under his arm. "Well, see you around," he said briefly, heading for the hall.

Miraculously, Sarah managed to find her voice. "I'm Sarah Connell," she yelled after him.

"Cody Rice," the boy replied. His voice gave her goose bumps. To cover her nervousness, she took another sip of hot chocolate and winced. She closed her eyes in pain, and when she opened them, he was gone.

She could hardly wait to find Micki and Matt. Her eyes were stinging, her mouth was on fire, and her throat was scorched. This had been the most wonderful five minutes of her entire life!

"Cody Rice? I don't know him," Micki said breezily an hour later. They were sitting side by side in Mr. Ferris's English class, waiting for the bell to ring. "But the name sounds familiar." She brushed a stray lock of red hair out of her eyes and peered at her friend. "What's he look like?"

"Like nobody else in the world," Sarah said, and Micki groaned.

"Please, give me a break!"

"All right," Sarah agreed. "He looks sort of like Rob Lowe. He's got really black hair and these big blue eyes that look right through you."

"Uh-huh."

"And his voice. . . ." Sarah stared dreamily off into space. "I'll never forget it as long as I live. It's low. And it reminds me a little of Bono from U2."

"He's Irish?" Micki asked, surprised.

"No, of course he's not Irish," Sarah

snapped. Honestly, there were times when Micki took everything too literally! "I said his *voice* reminded me of Bono, not his accent." She paused. "Anyway, I think he might be from Texas or Arizona. He was wearing these terrific faded jeans, and he looks like a cowboy."

Micki laughed. "Sarah, everybody in Southern California wears faded jeans."

"Not like he does," Sarah whispered, just as the bell rang, and Mr. Ferris scurried into the room.

Mr. Ferris was a thin, energetic man who was perpetually late and disorganized. Sarah had always thought of him as "Mr. Ferris the Friendly Ferret," because he had bright little eyes, and spent a lot of time shuffling through his briefcase.

Sarah sighed and opened her notebook. "Back to the real world," she muttered to herself.

"Sarah! You're here! How wonderful! Happy birthday!" Pamela Huntley enveloped Sarah in a giant bear hug when she stepped into Plates and Pages later that day.

"Hi, Aunt Pam," Sarah said, feeling happy and breathless all at the same time. Meeting Aunt Pam was a little like stepping into a friendly tornado. You knew you could be swept off your feet at any moment, but you wouldn't miss it for the world, because you just knew you'd end up someplace exciting. Her aunt was a tall, slender woman with jet-black hair that cascaded all the way down her back. She cheerfully described her taste in clothes as "early flea market," and today she wore a lacy white Victorian blouse with a delicate bronze cameo at the throat. Her long flowing skirt was a deep burgundy color and she had knotted a bright silk scarf around her waist as a belt.

"I've got your favorite tea all ready for you," she said, motioning for Sarah to take a seat at a tiny wrought-iron table she kept in the corner window of the shop. "See, I've already poured it. Citrus Sunset. And there's some of those nice wheat-germ bars to go with it."

As she pulled out two chairs with pink-and-white striped seats, half a dozen thin gold bracelets jingled on her arm. "Oh, and there are some cookies and tarts, and a few other goodies." She giggled girlishly. "Some extras I just couldn't resist for a party."

Sarah sipped the steaming tea. "How did you know when I'd get here?" she said, puzzled. "If I had been late, the tea would have been cold."

Aunt Pam smiled. "Well, then we just would

have had to have *iced* tea, wouldn't we?" She passed a basket of scones to Sarah, and cupped her chin in her hands, peering at her niece with her mysterious golden eyes. She was a beautiful woman in her thirties with large, almond-shaped eyes that made her look a little like a tigress. "Anyway," Aunt Pam said, stirring some honey in her tea, "I knew you'd be on time."

"You did?"

Her aunt nodded. "Don't you ever, um, know something, without really knowing that you know it?"

Sarah chuckled. "Funny you should say that. I had a couple of things happen to me today like that."

"Really?" Her aunt looked interested. "Tell me."

Sarah munched a buttered scone and wondered where to start. "Do you ever say something and wonder why you said it?"

"All the time," Pamela said wryly. "Yesterday, I told a salesperson I wanted to buy a silk scarf to use as a belt with this skirt, and then I said I'd buy half a dozen in different colors. But that's not important," Pam said breezily. "Tell me what happened to you."

As briefly as she could, Sarah told her the

story about Nicole and the lip gloss, and then launched right into the coincidence in the school cafeteria. "It was so funny, Aunt Pam. As soon as I said the word 'pizza,' they announced over the PA that that's what we were having for lunch!"

Pamela sat silently, occasionally fingering a large ring she always wore. Sarah had always been fascinated by the ring, which was a single stone in a delicate gold setting. It was impossible to say what kind of stone it was, because it seemed to change colors so often. Sometimes it was as green as a field of clover, and other times it was slate blue, like the ocean on a stormy day.

Pamela was silent until Sarah finished the story, and then Pam remarked slowly, "You just *knew* where the lip gloss was, is that right?"

"I guess I must have," Sarah agreed. "No one *told* me," Sarah laughed.

Pamela cut two wedges of pound cake. She looked at Sarah for a long moment and then reached over and patted Sarah's hand.

What does *that* mean? Sarah thought.

Chapter 3

"Have you thought about what you're going to wear to the Halloween Dance?" Micki asked Sarah as they walked to school the next day. It was a hot, humid morning, and Sarah knew her hair would turn to frizz before lunchtime.

"I haven't had a chance to think about it," Sarah confessed. "I know I *don't* want to wear my Casper the Friendly Ghost costume again."

"You have to admit it was easy to make," Micki reminded her. "Just an old sheet and two eyeholes."

Sarah made a face. "Yeah, and I nearly starved to death, if you remember. I didn't have anything to eat or drink all night."

Micki laughed. "I can't believe we forgot to put in slits so you could stick your arms out."

They stopped at a red light, and Micki did a

double take as a light blue sedan passed them. "Hey, that was Kirk Tanner," she said. "And he's riding to school *alone*."

"Hmmm, that's nice," Sarah said absently. The light changed, and she stepped briskly off the curb.

Micki stared at her in amazement. "Sarah, have you heard a word I've been saying?"

"Of course," Sarah said, slowing her pace a little. The warm air hit her like a slap in the face and she wished she hadn't worn her safari outfit. It had looked terrific when she'd put it together that morning — a crisp khaki bush jacket and pants with a knife-sharp crease in them. She'd added a cool melon tank top with some wooden jewelry she'd found at a flea market. Even Simon had given an appreciative whistle when she'd appeared at breakfast. But now the jacket, weighted down with fashionable shoulder pads, felt as heavy as a bulletproof vest, and Sarah was wilting by the minute.

"You seem pretty calm about the whole thing," Micki said. "I thought Kirk Tanner was the love of your life. Unrequited, of course," she added, teasing.

"Very funny," Sarah said, nudging her in the ribs. "Kirk is nice — "

"Nice!" Micki repeated. "He's not only the editor of the paper and a track star; but he's also cute, and smart, and one of the most popular guys around." She gave Sarah a shrewd look. "Uh-oh, you're not hung up on what's-his-name, the Mystery Man, are you?

"Cody Rice," Sarah said softly. "He's the most *fantastic* boy I've ever met. If you saw him, you'd know what I mean, Micki."

"One day it's Kirk Tanner and the next day it's Cody Rice." Micki shook her head in disgust. "You know something, Sarah Connell? You are the most fickle person I've ever met!"

"How cute. You're in costume a little early aren't you? The Halloween Dance isn't until Saturday," Allison Rogers purred as she slid into a seat next to Sarah a few hours later. The cafeteria was crowded, and a quick look around the table showed that everyone had boycotted the lunch special, a sandwich stuffed with gray Mystery Meat.

"Costume?" Sarah said cautiously. Whenever Allison Rogers showed her little white teeth like that, she was about to pounce like a hungry barracuda.

"Well, you're supposed to be Sheena of the Jungle, right?" Allison said innocently. Her glittery blue eyes raked over Sarah's safari outfit. "Either that or you just escaped from *Wild Kingdom*."

Sarah bit her lip and didn't answer. Allison never missed a chance to put someone down, and Sarah had realized that there was nothing personal about her cruel remarks — Allison disliked *everyone!*

"It's the safari look," Micki said indignantly. "If you ever read the fashion magazines, you'd know it was the latest thing."

"Well, excuuuuse me!" Allison said. She took a delicate sip of her iced tea and looked around the table. All girls, she thought wearily, except for Matt Neville, who didn't count. "I thought maybe she was tracking a herd of wildebeests."

She waited for the laugh, and when it didn't come, she turned to Tina Jordan. "So," she said, "do you want to hear what *I'm* going to wear to the dance?"

"I can hardly wait," Tina said in a sarcastic tone that temporarily silenced Allison.

Then everyone started talking about a French test, but Sarah was silent, thinking about the Halloween Dance. Would Cody be there? Probably, she thought. And with any luck he'd be there by himself. After all, she was almost positive he was new at Waterview

High, and he surely hadn't had time to meet anybody yet. Who am I kidding? He won't be alone for long, she thought wryly.

Her only hope was to wear such a dynamite costume to the dance, he just had to notice her!

The house was quiet when Sarah let herself in the back door after school that day. "Good, nobody's home yet," she said to Micki. She dropped her books on the kitchen table and walked to the connecting door that led to her father's suite of offices. She carefully cracked open the door and listened intently.

Then she closed it softly and said, "Three head colds, one case of croup, and a baby who sounds like she's got a diaper pin sticking in her."

"You can tell all that?"

Sarah nodded. "I've had years of practice. When I was little, I used to dream about having a soundproof bedroom."

"Really? I kind of like all the noise and confusion around here." She gave a wistful smile. "My house is so quiet, I catch myself talking to the plants."

"Well, whenever you feel like a little chaos, you know you're welcome here," Sarah told her. She knew that Micki was lonely sometimes. She didn't mind being an only child, but she was finding it difficult to adjust to her parents' divorce.

"So, where do we start?" Micki asked, looking around the sparkling kitchen.

"First we load up on carbohydrates, and then we head upstairs," Sarah said.

"Carbohydrates?" Micki looked uncomfortable. "Not those zucchini bars your father makes."

"No way." Sarah laughed. She opened a cabinet and wrestled briefly with a mountain of pots and pans. "I've got a secret supply tucked away back here," she said. "Unless Simon has gotten here first. Nope, here we go!" She held up a brown paper bag triumphantly. "Food fit for the gods, as Mr. Ferris would say."

"Nectar?"

"Of course not. Twinkies!"

"The way I see it, we have two choices," Micki said a few minutes later. "We can go for something traditional, or we can be really outrageous."

They were sitting on the floor in Sarah's room, surrounded by yards of fabric. Sarah loved to buy bolts of cloth at flea markets and discount stores. She wadded them in an overstuffed wicker trunk in the corner of her room and dragged them out whenever she felt like sewing.

"Outrageous," Sarah answered promptly. "Traditional sounds dull."

"Somehow I knew you'd say that," Micki said. In some ways, she and Sarah were exact opposites. Sarah impulsively put together outfits that no one else would think of, while Micki stuck to safe choices — quiet plaids and soft ruffles.

Sarah grinned. "Let's see, what's the first thing that comes to mind when you think of Halloween?"

"Pumpkins, I guess. Great, big, fat jack o' lanterns."

"Puh-leeze!" Sarah said. "Do you really think I want to go to the most important dance of my life dressed as a gourd?"

"You could wear your Casper costume," Micki teased her. "We could dye it orange." She ducked as Sarah pretended to be about to strangle her with an Indian macrame belt.

Simon knocked on the open door just then, and they turned in surprise. "Is this a private murder, or is it open to the public?"

"A friendly disagreement," Micki told him breathlessly. She tucked her gray twill skirt modestly around her legs and brushed her bright auburn hair out of her eyes. Sarah noticed that whenever Simon was around, Micki always perked up. Her eyes seemed brighter and she seemed to laugh more. She'd often wondered if her best friend was attracted to her brother, but she had never asked.

"What do you want, Simon? You're interrupting a brainstorming session here." Sarah fingered a bolt of shiny black vinyl. There must be *some* way to use it.

Simon ran his hand through his tousled blond hair and said quickly, "I just wondered if you had anything to eat up here. I spent two hours at track practice today and I'm starving."

"There's cold cuts in the fridge."

"I know, I just made a sandwich."

"Oh, honestly!" Sarah tossed him the Twinkie bag, and he peered inside.

"For me? How nice."

"It's a bribe," Sarah said flatly. "To leave."

"I'm on my way," Simon said, zigzagging his way across the room. He strummed an imaginary guitar as he headed for the hall. " 'And I won't be back for many a day . . .' " he sang in a loud, off-key voice.

"He's so funny," Micki said after he'd left.

"You think so?" Sarah wrinkled her nose.

"Now, let's get back to work." She held up the shiny black vinyl. "What do you think?"

"Perfect. All you need is a Harley-Davidson and a tattoo."

"Micki!"

"All right," Micki relented. "It's not bad, but what did you have in mind?"

"I don't know," Sarah said thoughtfully. "Not a ghost, not a ghoul . . ."

"Not a vampire," Micki offered.

"Definitely not. I'll leave that to Allison. She's got the fangs for it."

Sarah stared at the bolt of black vinyl and suddenly a shape started to emerge.

"A witch," she said abruptly. "I'm going as a witch. It's perfect! I don't know why I didn't see it before." She laughed delightedly and reached for a piece of chalk. She was so sure of her idea, she wasn't going to make a paper pattern first, like she usually did. She was going to draw the pattern with chalk and start cutting right then and there.

"A witch? As in pointy hat and broomstick?"

Sarah paused. "No, more like an unconventional witch. Kind of a hip witch. She dresses in black, but she belongs to the eighties."

Micki nodded agreeably. She didn't have a clue as to what Sarah was talking about, but she knew that once Sarah got started with scissors and pins, there would be no stopping her.

Sarah must have noticed Micki was quiet, because she said suddenly, "We can plan your costume while I'm cutting this one, Micki. I want you to have something terrific to wear, too."

Micki shrugged, watching Sarah's fingers fly over the bolt of vinyl. "I don't know where to start," she said a little shyly. "You're the creative one."

Sarah brushed away the compliment. "You're very creative, Micki," she told her. "Now, what would you really like to be?"

Micki thought for a minute. "Well, I've always wanted to be a cat. Does that sound too silly?"

Sarah looked up, her mouth full of pins, and nodded vigorously.

Micki looked worried. "Yes, it's a good idea? Or yes, it sounds silly?"

Sarah laughed and took the pins out of her mouth. "Yes, it's a good idea," she assured her. "As soon as I finish this, we're going to make you the most fantastic cat costume you've ever seen." She motioned to the wicker trunk. "I've got some furry tiger-print cotton in there that will look great on you."

"You think so? I hope I'm not making a mistake."

"You're not," Sarah said firmly. She tucked her legs more comfortably under her, and peered at her friend. "I've always known you would look great in whiskers!"

"It was so sweet of you to come over and help me," Aunt Pam said a couple of days later. "I really feel guilty dragging you out of bed on a Saturday morning. This is the one day you can sleep late."

"That's okay, Aunt Pam." Sarah yawned and looked around the crowded little shop. They wouldn't be open to the public for another hour, and it was just as well, Sarah thought sleepily. They were so many cardboard boxes jammed in the narrow aisles, that no one would be able to get to the shelves.

"It looks like you bought out a warehouse," Sarah said, opening the carton nearest her.

"Something like that. It was an estate sale." Aunt Pam bent down and carefully lifted a book out of the box. She blew a ribbon of dust off the leather binding and smiled at Sarah. "It's a beautiful collection, isn't it? The books are very old and fragile."

Sarah cracked open a book and sneezed.

"Elias Hirschorn?" she said, reading the flyleaf. "Was he somebody famous?"

"Probably not." Aunt Pam gave a wry smile. "The auctioneer told me that the owner of these books had a real knack for picking obscure authors." Aunt Pam pushed aside a beaded curtain in the rear of the shop that led to a tiny kitchen. "You know what I think we need? A nice hot cup of tea!"

"Sounds good to me," Sarah agreed. "I'll get started out here." As soon as her aunt disappeared behind the curtain, Sarah was seized with another sneezing fit. "These darn books make more dust than a cement mixer," she muttered, wiping her eyes. She bent down and looked at a few more titles. She had never heard of any of them.

"Lemon Zinger or Cranberry Delight?" Aunt Pam yelled.

"Lemon Zinger," Sarah answered in a wheezy voice. She must be allergic to the books, she decided. She reached for another book, tried to suppress a giant sneeze, and failed. At the rate she was going, she'd have red eyes and a runny nose for the Halloween Dance that night. She wouldn't need a costume — she'd be wearing her own fright mask!

And the boxes! There must be thirty of

them, she thought despairingly. They lined all four walls and the center aisle; it was going to take hours to unpack them. Sarah shut her eyes tightly, yawned, and stretched.

"I wish all these books were put away," she muttered.

When she opened her eyes, she reached down to start on the first pile of boxes, and drew back in surprise. It was gone! First she thought that she must have moved it, and then she wondered if she was dreaming. She *knew* there had been three large gray cartons, stacked on top of each other, piled right next to her feet. She remembered distinctly that the top box was labeled COOKBOOKS. And now the whole pile was gone.

She blinked quickly and looked again. Gone! It was *impossible*. Maybe she had made a mistake, and the pile was sitting in the next aisle. She ducked behind a row of paperbacks and scanned the aisle. It was empty.

"This is crazy," she muttered.

She slowly walked around the store, scanning the wooden shelves that towered to the ceiling. Suddenly she froze, her pulse hammering in her throat. The cookbook section was filled. It had been empty a few minutes before, she was positive. That's why she had decided to start unpacking the cookbooks first.

Sarah swallowed hard. She *must* be dreaming. She took a tiny fold of skin between her wrist and elbow and pinched hard.

It hurt.

She was awake.

"Calm down," she whispered. "There's got to be a logical explanation."

She walked quickly down another aisle, feeling her heart do a crazy drumbeat in her chest. There were dozens of boxes cluttering the store, but not that particular pile — not the cookbooks. Sarah looked at the shelves again. The cookbooks were still there, in brightly colored rows, and then suddenly something else caught her eye. The boxes! She caught a glimpse of them through the plate-glass door. There were three gray cardboard boxes outside, piled neatly at the curb next to a trash can. Sarah could tell from the way they were stacked together that they were empty.

"Of course they're empty!" she said aloud, and started to giggle, the way she always did when she got nervous. She ran her hand worriedly through her long brown hair. "What's going on?" she said aloud.

A voice behind her made her jump. "What did you say, Sarah?"

It was Aunt Pam. "Aunt Pam, Aunt Pam!" Sarah babbled. "Something crazy's going on here. The books. . . . There were some cartons of cookbooks here a moment ago. . . ."

"Yes?" Aunt Pam said calmly.

"And . . . now they're gone. *Gone!* I mean, they're all put away on the shelves. See, that section is filled." She clutched her aunt's arm as though it were a life preserver. "Look! Look!"

Aunt Pam dutifully turned and looked at the neatly arranged shelves.

"Yes, I see that. It's very nice."

Sarah stared at her, her eyes wide with shock. "But how can that be? The boxes were here just a minute ago. I hadn't touched them yet! And now they're empty . . . out at the curb. Am I going crazy? Am I imagining things?"

"Sshhh, it's all right, dear." Aunt Pam took Sarah by both arms and looked into her eyes. "You're not going crazy and you're not imagining things. There's something you need to know, and I guess this is the time to tell you."

"Tell me?" Sarah shouted. "Tell me *what?*"

Aunt Pam's golden eyes softened and there was a slight hesitation before she spoke.

"I have some exciting news for you, Sarah."

She smiled warmly. "You have wonderful powers that you don't even know about."

"What are you saying? Are you trying to tell me that I somehow managed to put the books on the shelves."

Aunt Pam paused. "Something like that."

"Just by wishing it?" Sarah said.

"Something like that," Aunt Pam repeated.

"The lip gloss and the pizza?" Sarah said. "Are they all part of this?"

Aunt Pam nodded. "It's all part of the same thing, Sarah. This is just the beginning."

Chapter 4

Maybe the room started to spin. Or maybe the room was standing still and Sarah was the one who was whirling in circles. It was impossible to say, but the next thing she knew, Aunt Pam was gently pushing her into a chair.

"Oh, dear," Aunt Pam said worriedly. "It's always a bit of a shock, but once you get a chance to adjust to the idea — "

"It must be a joke," Sarah said. "A trick of some sort." She looked blankly around the shop. "Did you do it with mirrors?"

"Mirrors?" Aunt Pam giggled, and her laughter reminded Sarah of a dozen little silver bells. "Of course not, Sarah. I told you, I didn't do it at all. *You did.*"

"*I* put the books away?" Sarah repeated incredulously.

"You must have," her aunt said, sitting down across from her. "If you think back for a moment, you'll realize I'm right. Now, what happened right before the, uh, incident?"

Sarah took a deep breath and let it out slowly. "Well," she said, "I was tired, so I yawned and stretched." She frowned for a moment, remembering. "And I remember saying to myself that I wished the books were all back on the shelves."

"*Aha!*" Aunt Pam said triumphantly. "One of your first acts as an apprentice. Congratulations, Sarah!"

An apprentice? What in the world was Aunt Pam talking about? An apprentice *what?*

Sarah stared. "Aunt Pam," she said firmly, "tell me the truth! Tell me what really happened to the books! And tell me why you called me an apprentice."

"Sarah," her aunt said, "look at me." Sarah obediently turned to her aunt and found herself staring into those incredible golden eyes. "Have I ever lied to you?"

Sarah shook her head. "No," she admitted.

"And I'm not lying now." She paused to let the words sink in. "You're thirteen now, and it's time for you to know these things. As it turned out, you discovered the truth by accident . . . but if you hadn't, I would have told you anyway. Thirteen is the time to be told."

Sarah just sat totally still. Waiting.

"That's when my mother told me," Aunt Pam said happily. "I remember how excited I was — "

"Aunt Pam!" Sarah pleaded. "Will you please tell me *what* you're talking about? And you can start by telling me why you said I was an apprentice."

"Oh, dear, it's so hard to find the right words." Aunt Pam stalled. "All right, I'll do my best to explain this to you. I called you an apprentice, because it means you're a beginner, a student."

"A student of *what*?"

"At being a witch, of course."

"A witch!" Sarah shouted. "But that's impossible. I don't know anything about being a witch."

"Oh, yes, you do," Aunt Pam said. "You know more than you think. And as time goes on, with some study and hard work, you'll learn the full extent of your powers."

"The full extent of my powers. . . ." Sarah's eyes widened. "You don't mean, you can't mean that I'm. . . ." Her voice trailed off.

"You're a witch, Sarah," her aunt said, smiling. She tucked a lock of raven hair behind her ear. "And, of course, I am, too." She nodded vigorously. "We're like sisters, you and I, Sarah. That's why there has always been this wonderful bond between us. You can feel it, can't you?"

Sarah swallowed hard, trying to find her voice. "Is this a joke? Maybe you're doing this because of Halloween — is that it? I *mean* . . . a *witch?*"

"Sarah," Aunt Pam said, "do you really think I would play a joke on you? That I would tease you about something like this?"

"I . . . I don't know what to think," Sarah admitted. "But I can't think of any other explanation."

"Why not the obvious explanation?" Aunt Pam said gently. "That I'm telling you the truth."

If Aunt Pam *was* telling the truth, it was even more confusing than she had imagined. Sarah said, "You must be wrong. I mean, in this day and age . . . a witch!" Sarah grabbed her jacket and walked down the aisle.

"Sarah, come back!" Her aunt reached out her hand to stop her, but Sarah went toward the front door.

"I need some fresh air, Aunt Pam. I'll . . .

I'll talk to you later." Under her breath she mumbled, "Witch?" Once outside, she raced up Market Street and didn't stop running until she had put five blocks between herself and Plates and Pages. Then, she stopped, leaned against a building, and took in several deep gulps of air.

Aunt Pam couldn't be telling the truth, could she? There was that incident with the lip gloss, of course, and the pizza . . . and today. . . . There was simply no logical explanation for what had happened to the books.

Unless, she *did* have some magic powers. Would that make her a witch? That was *impossible!* Sarah took another deep breath. She'd have to get home and think this through. Was she really Sarah Connell . . . teen witch?

Nicole looked up in surprise when Sarah ran in the house half an hour later. "Back so soon?" she asked idly. "I thought you were going to help Aunt Pam this morning." Nicole was sitting alone at the breakfast table, and she motioned for Sarah to sit with her. "Want some bran muffins? Dad made them." She laughed. "But don't hold that against them. They're actually pretty good. I think he forgot to add the bran."

"I can't eat," Sarah blurted out. "I can't even sit down. I'm too . . . upset." She paced the kitchen while Nicole watched her curiously. Her hands felt like lumps of ice. If her father saw her, he'd say she had a fever, but Sarah knew better.

"What's wrong?" Nicole asked, popping a piece of muffin in her mouth.

Sarah opened her mouth to answer, and then closed it abruptly. How could she tell anyone this crazy story? They'd roll on the floor laughing, and then they'd lock her up! She looked at Nicole, so cool and thoughtful. She'd never understand in a million years . . . and yet, Sarah had to tell *someone!*

She slid into her chair and stared at her sister. "Nicole," she whispered. "The strangest thing has happened."

"Are you all right?" Nicole said, peering at her. "You look weird."

Sarah leaned forward until her face was just inches from her sister's. "Look, I don't *want* to be a witch!"

Nicole pondered this for a moment, and then calmly reached for the comics. "So don't be," she said calmly.

Sarah stared at her sister. "What?"

"*Don't* be a witch," Nicole repeated. She

reached for the steaming tea kettle and filled two cups. Then she pushed one toward Sarah and said cheerfully, "I always thought witch and black cat costumes were kind of overdone for Halloween anyway. If you ask me, I think you should try something different tonight. Maybe go as a ballerina, or wear a black tuxedo and go as Charlie Chaplin. Something . . . imaginative."

Sarah giggled in surprise. Nicole thought she was talking about her witch *costume!* "You don't understand — " she began, and was cut off when Simon plopped into the seat next to her.

"If we're talking Halloween costumes, I've got a fantastic idea," he said. "How about the Jolly Green Giant?" Nicole groaned and he held up his hand. "Now wait a minute. Just hear me out. A guy at school did it last year, and he looked great. You start with a green body suit, and then you take a couple of bushels of leaves and glue them on, one by one — "

Sarah jumped to her feet. "Wait a minute! You don't understand what I'm talking about! It's not funny! I don't want to be a witch!" She stood there, her hands on her hips, glaring at them, while they looked at her in amazement.

"Well, aren't *we* touchy today?" Simon kidded her. At that moment, her mother appeared. "What's going on here?" she asked.

"Sarah," Simon said helpfully, "really freaked out."

"She says she doesn't want to be a witch," Nicole volunteered. "Honestly, Sarah, it's only a high school dance. It's not the end of the world."

"Sarah, dear, tell me what's wrong." Mrs. Connell's voice was low and soothing. "Does it have something to do with the dance tonight? If you'd like, I'll help you make a new costume."

Sarah held up a hand. "That's not it at all. I just wish it were that simple," she said. "Listen. . . ."

Mrs. Connell looked puzzled. "I think your witch costume is lovely."

"Yeah, it's kind of cute, Sarah," Simon said. "All that black vinyl. It makes you look like Mad Max."

"Simon," Mrs. Connell said reproachfully. "This is no time for jokes." She turned back to Sarah. "Now, dear, if you'll just tell me what's wrong, I know we can straighten it out."

"That's what *you* think," Sarah said. "Nothing in the world can straighten *this* out." She shook her head, shrugged, and then ran up to her room.

Slamming the door behind her, she threw herself on the bed, and hugged Bandit, the family's black and white cat, who was half buried under the quilt. "What can I do?" she said to Bandit. "No one will ever believe what's happening to me."

After a few moments, she calmed down and sat up. The immediate problem, she decided, was what to do about the dance that night. Everyone in the family would expect her to act normal. How could she act normal? She'd just had the biggest surprise of her life! And anyway, how does a witch act normal? What is a *normal* witch?

Then the next problem would be how to get through the Halloween Dance. The last thing in the world she wanted to do was dress up as a witch, but how could she cancel? What would she tell Micki?

She stretched out in bed, her hands behind her head. It was almost funny, she thought. Here she was, worrying about the Halloween Dance, when she should be wondering what to do about the rest of her life.

A light tap at the door made her jump. The door opened, and her father stuck his head around the corner. "Thought I'd look in on the patient," he kidded her.

Sarah smiled. "I'm not a patient," Sarah reminded him. "I'm not even sick."

Dr. Connell sat on the edge of the bed and said with mock seriousness, "That's not the way I hear it. I heard you're suffering from post-birthday blues."

He tickled her under the chin, the way he always did to make her laugh, and Sarah had to chuckle. She longed to throw her arms around him and tell him what had happened. But how could she find the words? Dad, your daughter is a teenage witch, but don't get upset.

"Not exactly," Sarah said.

"No?" Her father touched her forehead. "Then maybe you're running a fever, or have the flu . . . or even malaria. You haven't been spending much time in the jungle, have you?"

"Not that I know of." They used to go through this routine when Sarah was a little girl. By the time they finished, Sarah always felt much better. It was funny, she thought, her father had a way of making you laugh through any situation.

"Nicole says you're unhappy with your costume," he said casually. "Anything I can do to help?"

Sarah smiled at him again. "I don't think so.

I've changed my mind. I think I was making too big a deal about it."

"And you're sure nothing's wrong?" He looked at her closely.

"I'll survive," she said wryly. The phone beside her bed rang just then, and Sarah hesitated. "That's probably Micki. . . ."

Her father stood up, looking relieved. "Well, I don't want to interrupt your conversation," he teased her. "You've probably got a lot of things to discuss before the dance."

"Thanks, Dad." Sarah tried to look reassuring. "We do."

She waited till the door closed before snatching the receiver off the hook. "Micki?" she said breathlessly.

"Yes, but how did you know?" Micki sounded puzzled. "You must be a psychic!"

"A lucky guess," Sarah told her. If only she knew the truth!

"Are you excited about tonight?" Micki's voice bubbled over the line. "I've been trying on my cat costume all afternoon. Mom says if I wear it in the kitchen one more time, she's going to kill me. She almost closed my tail in the refrigerator door!" She paused. "You did a fantastic job on it, Sarah. I can't believe how talented you are."

"I'm glad you like it," Sarah said vaguely. She tried to concentrate on what Micki was saying, but it was difficult. Her mind kept racing back to that startling, unbelievable scene with Aunt Pam in the bookstore. She could still see those piles of books, neatly arranged on the shelves . . . as if by magic. But of course! It *was* magic, she thought. She shook her head, as if to clear it, as Micki rambled on.

"I'm pretty sure that most people are going as singles tonight, so that leaves the door wide open for you and Kirk Tanner."

"Uh-huh."

"And as for me . . . well, I guess the whole school is up for grabs!" Micki chuckled, and waited for Sarah to join in. When there was dead silence on the other end of the line, she said impatiently, "Honestly, Sarah, what's wrong with you today? Talking to you is like talking to a stick."

"I'm sorry," Sarah apologized. "I . . . I just have a lot on my mind, I guess."

"Did your costume turn out all right?" Micki asked with concern. "I thought it was perfect for you. You really *look* like a witch."

"So they tell me," Sarah muttered. "Look," she said hastily, "do you mind if I talk to you later? I've got tons of stuff to do before the dance."

"Sure," Micki agreed, a little surprised. "Will you still have time to do my makeup?"

"Of course." Sarah glanced at the clock. "Just get over here around seven." As she hung up the phone, she accidentally jostled Bandit, who complained with a loud meow.

"Sorry, Bandit," she murmured. She rearranged his pillow, and then gave him a long hug. He lazily flipped over on his back, allowed her to rub his stomach, and then drifted back to sleep. Sarah watched him for a moment. "I wish my life could be as simple as yours," she said enviously.

She swung her legs over the bed and stared at herself in the mirror. She still *looked* the same. Her creamy skin was a little paler than usual, but the sparkling brown eyes and long dark hair looked normal. Except of course, she *wasn't* normal. She was a witch! A witch? No one in their right mind would consider *that* normal.

"If you don't hold still, your whiskers will be off-center," Sarah warned. It was seven-thirty, and she was putting the finishing touches on Micki's makeup.

"My neck hurts," Micki complained. She was sitting on Sarah's bed, with her head tilted up toward the ceiling light.

"I'm almost finished," Sarah told her. She wielded a tiny brush and drew thin lines outward from Micki's nose. She had covered Micki's face with a tawny shade of liquid makeup she'd borrowed from Nicole, and had given her big cat-eyes and a round button nose. "I still think we should have spray-painted your hair," she said, stepping back to examine her work.

"No!" Micki protested. "My mom would have a fit. I'll look fine this way."

"A few orange streaks would have been nice," Sarah said, touching Micki's hair. It was teased in a fluffy red mane around her face, giving her a startled, almost comic look. "I know, how about a few gold sparkles?"

"Sparkles?"

Sarah nodded and searched in her closet for a jar of glitter. "It will add some highlights," she said, tossing a handful on Micki's head. "And it will wash right out."

"Highlights? It'll look too punk."

"No, it will look just right, you'll see," Sarah encouraged. "Close your eyes and don't open them till I tell you to," she ordered, pulling

Micki to the mirror. "I want you to get the full effect all at once."

A moment later, Micki opened her eyes and gasped in surprise. "I can't believe it!" She peered in the mirror and saw a cat face staring back at her.

"Do you like it?" Sarah stood next to her, watching her friend's expression in the mirror.

"Like it? I love it! You're a genius. And this costume . . ." Micki turned from side to side admiring the sleek jumpsuit Sarah had made out of the tiger print cotton. "I'm going to save it and wear it next year." She leaned over and impulsively hugged Sarah. "You're the best friend in the whole world," she said. "Hey, look at us — we make quite a pair, don't we?" she added, glancing in the mirror. "A tiger and a witch."

Every time Sarah looked at herself in her black vinyl witch costume, she gasped. Where's my broom? she thought. Don't witches have brooms?

"This is going to be the best night of my life," Micki said, dragging Sarah back to the present.

"I hope so," Sarah said. She took a deep breath. She was determined not to ruin the Halloween Dance for Micki. The best thing to do was to relax and enjoy herself tonight.

There would be plenty of time afterward to face the truth. . . . And maybe tomorrow she'd be an ex-witch. Who knew?

A few minutes later, she and Micki emerged into the living room to a chorus of applause. "Fantastic costumes," Dr. Connell said, while Simon gave a low wolf whistle.

"You both look terrific," Mrs. Connell said, walking them to the front door. "Have a good time tonight."

"Oh, we will, Mrs. Connell," Micki said. "Sarah will be lucky tonight."

"Lucky tonight?" Sarah repeated.

Micki laughed. She pointed to the long red banner that Mrs. Connell had hung from the ceiling on the day of Sarah's birthday and was still up.

Sarah looked at it and had to stifle a laugh. The banner said: HAPPY BIRTHDAY, LUCKY 13. She ducked her head quickly, before her expression could give her away. "Let's go," Sarah said quickly. "This witch doesn't want to be late for the dance."

Chapter 5

"I just hope no one steps on my tail tonight," Micki said a little later, as she and Sarah dashed up the stone steps to the Waterview High School gymnasium.

"You better wrap it around your hand when you dance," Sarah instructed her. "Otherwise you'll end up being a Manx cat instead of a tiger."

"I'll try to remember," Micki said breathlessly. "Wow, listen to that band!" The heavy beat of a rock song drifted through the open doors, piercing the cool night air.

Sarah grinned. "Loud enough to loosen your fillings, as my father would say."

They turned in their tickets to a smiling junior dressed in a sleek black vampire suit, and made their way to the buffet table. The gymnasium was mobbed with kids, and the dark blue strobe lights gave the whole scene an eerie, otherworld feeling. It was a strange night, a night when anything could happen, Sarah thought a little nervously. It was impossible to tell who was who behind the wild costumes, and even the two teacher-chaperones were wearing fright masks.

"Sarah! You look fantastic!" Sarah turned to see a grinning death's head next to her and almost jumped out of her skin. "I bet you made your costume yourself; it's the neatest one here."

"Oh, it's you, Heather," Sarah said, finding her voice.

"Well, of course it's me!" Heather Larson giggled.

"Who's here tonight?" Sarah said, scanning the crowd.

"Just about everyone," Heather told her. "Tina Jordan came as a scarecrow. Look, she's over by the basketball hoop, the one with the straw sticking out of her sleeves, and Beverly Dobson came as Dorothy from *The Wizard of Oz*. She's holding that little stuffed dog and dancing with Kirk Tanner," she added, watching Sarah's face. When Sarah didn't say anything, Heather turned to Micki. "I heard she had a thing for Kirk."

Micki shrugged. "Not anymore. She's into cowboys."

"Cowboys?" Heather looked over the dance floor. "I don't think I've seen anyone dressed like that."

"Oh, it's not a costume," Micki said, sneaking a look at Sarah. "This guy she met just likes to dress like that . . . he wears spurs to school. He probably parks his steer in the bike rack."

"Micki!" Sarah objected. "She's kidding," she explained to Heather.

Heather took a closer look at Sarah's black vinyl costume. "You look great," she said admiringly. "You look just like a real witch!"

Sarah eyes widened at the words. She started to reply when a silky voice cut her short.

"Well, well," Allison Rogers said snidely, "it must be girls' night out." She looked at Sarah, Micki, and Heather clustered around the buffet table, and then her piercing eyes settled on Sarah's outfit. "Hey, didn't you forget something?" she cackled. "Where's your broomstick?"

"This is the eighties," Sarah said coolly. "We take the Concorde now. What are you dressed as?"

"Obviously, I'm a fairy princess." Allison

flushed and gulped her Coke. She always hated it when anyone upstaged her. She was staring hard at Sarah, trying to think of another nasty remark, when Matt Neville wandered over. With him was Erin Chambers, a very tall, shy girl who was so nearsighted she always wore thick glasses. As usual, she was slumped over, trying to disguise her height.

Sarah glanced at Allison and could practically see the wheels clicking in her head, as she pondered her next attack. Since she was such an easy victim, Erin was always the butt of Allison's cruelest jokes.

"Hey, you two didn't even need costumes tonight," Allison said, her eyes glinting with laughter. "You could be Mutt and Jeff." She let her eyes travel slowly from Erin's feet to her head, and then she reeled backward in surprise, as if she were surveying the Empire State Building.

"Honestly, Allison," Micki said, annoyed. Her heart went out to Erin, who practically buckled at the knees, trying to look shorter. Unfortunately, Erin had chosen the world's worst costume. She was wearing a plaid Scottish kilt with knee socks, a combination that made her look twice as tall. A pair of bagpipes hung limply from her neck like an albatross, and she looked sad and discouraged.

"Oh, Erin doesn't mind a little kidding, do you?" Allison goaded her. "I'm sure she's used to it." She waved to someone across the room. "See you later," she said sweetly, and moved off.

"I certainly hope not," Micki said feelingly. "Wouldn't it be nice if the dance floor would just open and swallow her up?"

"Don't count on it," Matt told her. "People like Allison are like kryptonite. They're indestructible!" He looked at Heather and grinned. "I think they're playing our song," he said as "Thriller" blasted over the loudspeaker. "Want to dance?"

"I'd love to," Heather told him, and they linked arms and headed for the dance floor.

"I think I'll go talk to the chaperones," Erin said quickly. "Maybe they'd like me to bring them something to drink."

"Wait a minute, we'll go with you," Micki offered, but Erin had already vanished into the crowd, her silly bagpipes still hanging around her neck.

"Poor Erin," Sarah said sympathetically. "She probably thought we didn't want to talk to her."

"I know, it's a shame. She's really a nice girl.

All she needs is a little self-confidence."

"She'll never get it as long as Allison keeps putting her down," Sarah said.

This is going to be the strangest night of my life, Sarah thought. She knew she couldn't hide at the buffet table forever, but the last thing she wanted to do was join the throng of people on the dance floor. If one more person says I look just like a witch, I'll scream, she said silently.

"What next?" Micki said brightly.

Sarah knew she was dying to dance. "There's Jeff Tyson over there," she pointed out. "He's just standing at the edge of the dance floor, tapping his foot. Why don't you . . . ?"

"Ask him to dance?" Micki said eagerly. "Do you think I should?" Her brown eyes sparkled with excitement.

Sarah laughed. "Hey, you're the king of the jungle, you can do what you want tonight."

Micki frowned. "I think the king of the jungle is the lion, not the tiger."

"Believe me," Sarah assured her. "When Jeff sees you in your tiger costume, he won't care a bit."

A few minutes later, Sarah found herself alone in the girls' room, looking at her reflection in the mirror. She'd darted inside to run a brush through her brown hair, but the green-tiled room was cool and quiet. Any other time, she would have been in the middle of the dance floor, laughing and joking with her friends, maybe even searching the crowd for Cody.

But tonight . . . everything was different. She wasn't just Sarah Connell, an average, well, maybe, better-than-average, thirteen-year-old anymore.

She was Sarah Connell, *teen witch!*

"I don't think I *look* any different," she said to the mirror. "Do I?"

She did a quick inventory. A tangle of hair that refused to be tamed, dark eyes that had a slightly quizzical look, a sprinkling of freckles on a cheerfully upturned nose. An ordinary face, she thought, and then she laughed.

"Is this what an ordinary witch looks like?" she said aloud. "Do witches have *freckles?*"

"Talking to yourself?" Micki's voice boomed from the door.

"I just came in to . . ." Sarah faltered.

"To admire your costume one more time," Micki said with a laugh. "That's okay. You're entitled. You've got the best costume here. But that's not why I came to get you," Micki said meaningfully.

"What's up?" Sarah said, instantly alert. She knew Micki well enough to know that something was wrong.

"It's Erin," Micki said softly. "Allison is making mincemeat out of her. Every time I leave Erin alone, Allison goes in for the kill. Do you think you could — "

"You bet I could!" Sarah said, brushing past Micki and heading for the gymnasium.

"What are you wearing the stupid things for, if you can't play them?" Allison was saying loudly to Erin as they stood by the punch bowl. A crowd had gathered around the two girls, and Erin looked as if she wanted to drop through the floor.

"I told you," she said in a quavery voice. "They're my brother's bagpipes."

Allison hooted. "I suppose that's his kilt, too?" She looked at Micki and Sarah, who were now standing next to Matt. "Hey, I've always wondered, what do you wear under those things?"

"Please . . ." Erin said, embarrassed. She turned to leave, but Allison was too fast for her. "I asked you a question," Allison said slyly. "Don't you think it would be polite to answer?" She looked at the crowd and winked.

"On the other hand, we could find out for ourselves. . . ."

Sarah stood frozen to the spot, watching the cruel little drama unfold. She guessed what was coming, and she knew that Erin would be so humilated she'd never be able to face anyone again.

The next few seconds seemed to happen in slow motion. Sarah was staring at Allison, who was clutching her punch glass tightly in her right hand, and her magic wand in her left. Allison reached out the wand and had barely moved the hem of Erin's kilt when she drew back with a scream.

"Oh, no!" Allison cried, staring at her snowy costume. "My dress!" The whole front of her dress was stained with grape punch, and the glass she was holding was empty. For a moment, everyone was stunned, and then they started laughing. At Allison.

"Hey, way to go!" a boy shouted, as Allison dabbed furiously at the front of her dress with a paper napkin.

"It's ruined," Allison said angrily. She flashed a look of pure malice at the crowd, and just for a moment, her eyes locked with Sarah's.

Sarah tried to keep her face expressionless,

but her heart jumped in her chest. *What* was going on? Had *she* caused the purple punch to spill all over Allison's dress? All she had done was look at it. She hadn't even *wished* it would happen! Or had she? Was it a crazy coincidence? Was it magic?

"Craziest thing I've ever seen," Matt was saying a minute later. Allison had vanished to the girls' room, and he and Micki and Sarah were still standing in a knot by the punch bowl. "I saw the whole thing," he said, lifting off his gorilla head and brushing his brown hair off his forehead.

"It was an accident," Micki said lightly. "Allison just spilled her drink all over herself. And it served her right, too," she said, lowering her voice. The band had struck up one of her favorite songs by the Stones and she was dying to dance. Why couldn't everyone forget about Allison and her stupid dress!

"Nope," Matt said firmly. "That's the funny thing. It wasn't an accident. It was more like — "

"Why don't we dance?" Micki said impatiently. "We're wasting some fantastic music."

"It certainly defied the law of physics," Matt said thoughtfully. "You see, I was standing right next to her. The glass actually tipped over by itself." He was still talking as Micki dragged him to the dance floor.

"Fascinating," Micki said. She reached for his gorilla head and plunked it over his ears. "You know something, Matt? I think I like you better this way!"

Sarah stood still for a moment, too surprised to talk to anybody. She had the sneaking suspicion that she *had* caused the grape punch to tip over. She felt a funny little chill go up her spine, as if someone were tickling her back with a feather. If she could do something like that . . . then she really did have magical powers. And she really *was* a witch.

It would be very strange, wouldn't it? Would she like it? Suddenly she remembered Allison's cruel smile when she was taunting Erin, and then her look of sheer horror when the grape punch spilled all over her. Of course it had been satisfying to see Allison get what she deserved. But the idea she had caused it was too weird. If she really *was* a witch, and she could do things like make grape juice spill on Allison Rogers, well . . . life could be quite amazing!

What *else* could she do?

Chapter 6

"Are you ready to put the light out yet?" Micki asked sleepily a few hours later. She glanced over at Sarah, who was curled up in the guest bed with the blanket tucked tightly under her chin. They were watching the midnight *Creep Feature*, and Sarah's eyes were glued to the screen. A vampire was tiptoeing down a palace corridor when he suddenly stubbed his toe against a suit of armor. A metal helmet skittered across the stone floor, and Sarah gasped.

"Careful, they'll hear you," Sarah hissed, staring at the TV. Seconds later, there was the sound of running feet, and the burly figure of a palace guard was silhouetted in an open doorway. "What did I tell you!" Sarah cried, biting her fingernails. "Quick, duck behind the curtains!"

"Sarah," Micki said impatiently, "whose side are you on, anyway?"

Sarah waited until the vampire had darted safely behind a tapestry before saying sheepishly, "You know I'm always for the underdog."

The film cut to a commercial just then, and she turned to her friend. "I'm glad you invited me to stay over tonight. It's hard to watch *Creep Feature* at home — Nicole and Simon always vote to watch a comedy show." She grinned. "They say I get too wrapped up in horror movies."

"You do!" Micki agreed with a laugh. "You're the only person I know who would root for a dinosaur that tried to eat Manhattan."

Sarah nodded. "I cried when Megalon died."

"I remember," Micki said, rolling her eyes. "Want some more popcorn?"

"I'm not hungry," Sarah said, causing Micki to look at her suspiciously.

"Are you sure you're not sick?" She swung her feet over the edge of the bed and peered at her friend. "You've turned down marshmallow brownies, double chocolate-chip ice cream, and lemon pound cake."

"I'm fine," Sarah said. She chose her words carefully. "I guess I'm still a little . . . excited over the dance tonight." Excited wasn't the word for it, she thought to herself. Tonight had been a real eye-opener. She had seen what being a witch meant. She felt a little chill every time she remembered the scene with the grape punch. She wondered for the dozenth time how she could ever break the news to Micki.

"Wow, it was really something," Micki said, hugging her pillow to her chest. "I'll never forget the look on Allison's face when the grape juice spilled all over her dress. In fact, I was just going to — "

"Sssh, the movie's back on!" Sarah interrupted her. They watched silently until the closing credits, and Micki reached for the remote-control.

"Now can I turn it off?" she asked, stifling a giant yawn.

"Just one more minute," Sarah pleaded. "I want to see what I'll be missing next week."

"You're impossible," Micki muttered. "Hey," she said, looking at the screen, "it's a movie about witches."

"Witches!" Sarah shouted.

"Looks pretty crazy to me," Micki snorted. She watched for a moment, and then pushed a button, and the screen went dark. She flopped back into bed and turned off the light. "'Night," she said, already starting to drift off to sleep.

"Micki," Sarah said urgently. Her voice seemed loud in the suddenly darkened room. "Wouldn't it be funny if some of this stuff was really true? Have you ever thought about it?"

"What stuff do you mean?" Micki mumbled, burying her face in her pillow.

"Oh, you know," Sarah said impatiently. "If there really *were* witches, and they really *had* magic powers."

Micki chuckled. "Your family's right. You've been watching too many horror movies."

"No, I'm serious," Sarah said, sitting up in bed. She scrunched the pillow behind her head and stared at a little sliver of moonlight that snaked in under the curtains. "Think how weird it would be . . . think of all the possibilities!"

"Uh-huh."

"Let's see . . ." Sarah said, wrapping her arms around her knees. "You could change things and make them go your own way. . . . You could imagine something, and bingo, it would appear right in front of you." She snapped her fingers. "Wouldn't it scare you a little?"

"It sounds great to me," Micki said, half-awake.

"But what if you made a mistake?" Sarah

said thoughtfully. "What if you wished for the wrong thing, and it came true and you were stuck with it?" She stared out the window, trying to collect her thoughts. "It would probably be really hard to undo it, and you might get in a lot of trouble."

"Uh-huh," Micki murmured.

"Of course there are two sides to everything," Sarah went on. "You could do a lot of things to help people, and you'd always know what was going to happen next . . . at least I *think* you would," she added doubtfully. Actually, she wasn't at all sure about that last part. Being a witch was obviously a lot more complicated than she had imagined, and there were probably all sorts of things she'd need to learn.

"Too bad it's just in the movies," Micki said, bringing Sarah down to earth with a jolt.

"What?" Sarah asked, still caught up in her fantasies.

"I said it's too bad that stuff like that just happens in the movies," Micki murmured.

"You mean witches?" Sarah offered.

Micki gave a loud yawn. "Witches, ghosts, ghouls, vampires. . . . What is it they call it? Things that go bump in the night."

"You're saying there's no chance they're real — not even witches?"

Micki chuckled and turned over. "Face it, Sarah. There's about as much chance of a witch appearing in this room as . . . that giant moth in that last movie we saw."

"That was Mothra!" Sarah said indignantly. "He was terrific."

"He ate a subway train in Toyko."

"He didn't mean to hurt anybody. He was just lost and confused," Sarah explained. "If somebody were attacking you with Howitzers, you wouldn't be thinking clearly, either." She paused, waiting for Micki to reply. "Right?" she said softly.

When there was no answer but the sound of Micki's breathing, Sarah shrugged and tucked her pillow under her head. It was very late, but she knew it would take a long time to fall asleep. There was so much to think about! She smiled, remembering the way the grape juice had splattered all over Allison's white dress. As if by magic.

It *was* magic, she reminded herself. *Her* magic. It was exciting and scary, all at the same time. And now she had to learn how to use it. She hoped Aunt Pam would be there for her, because she had a million questions that needed to be answered.

She was a witch!

The possibilities were fantastic. She could hardly *wait* to find out more!

The next morning was bright and clear, and Sarah jumped out of bed, eager to start the day. Was it her imagination, or did she feel just a little bouncier than usual? She glanced in the mirror: same mop of brown hair, same chocolate-drop eyes. She took a step closer to the mirror. Maybe the mouth was a little different, she decided. Yes, that was it. It seemed to twitch a little at the corners, as if she were caught in a perpetual smile.

And no wonder! She thought of a poster she had seen in a gift store. It said: TODAY IS THE FIRST DAY OF THE REST OF YOUR LIFE. It could have been written just for her!

She took a quick shower, and then burrowed in her overnight case for a pair of clean jeans and a T-shirt. Micki stirred in her sleep, and Sarah looked guiltily at the clock. Seven-thirty. A terrible time to wake someone up on Sunday morning. Maybe the best thing to do was leave a note and tiptoe out the door. She could call

Micki later and explain. She had to get over to Aunt Pam's.

Moments later, she was walking along Front Street, watching the early morning sunlight sparkle on the whitewashed buildings. She hummed softly to herself, swinging the overnight case lightly at her side. It was going to be a terrific day, she could feel it.

Plates and Pages was closed at this hour, but she gave her special ring on the buzzer — one long and three shorts, and Aunt Pam appeared at the door almost immediately. She looked beautiful, even early in the morning, and was wearing a pale yellow running suit that seemed to pick up the flecks of gold in her eyes.

"Sarah!" she said warmly, and threw her arms around her. "I knew you'd be here today."

She ushered her inside, and as usual, Sarah felt completely at home. The wonderful thing about Aunt Pam was that she just seemed to *know* how Sarah felt. There was no need to apologize for her leaving so abruptly the previous day . . . no need to explain why she had suddenly turned up on her doorstep. And Sarah was relieved that she didn't feel nervous or strange around her favorite aunt. Things actually seemed as if they were back to normal.

If you can call being a witch normal! Sarah thought wryly.

"You're just in time for breakfast," Aunt Pam said, leading the way upstairs to her apartment. The apartment was connected to the shop by a winding, black, wrought-iron staircase and was exactly the kind of place Sarah wanted to have when she grew up.

It was light and airy, with wide plank floors and dozens of cushions everywhere in every shade of the rainbow.

Aunt Pam motioned for her to sit down at the long butcher-block table, and began pouring tea. "So tell me all about last night," she said cheerfully. "Oh, put him on the floor if he bothers you," she added as Grumble, her temperamental Siamese, jumped into Sarah's lap.

"That's okay, I like him," Sarah said, stroking the cat's silky fur. He made a deliriously happy noise deep in his throat, and started purring like an outboard motor. "How did you know about last night?" she asked in surprise.

Aunt Pam smiled. "Sheer instinct." When Sarah raised her eyebrows, she explained. "You seem very different than when you left here yesterday," she said reasonably. "Therefore, something must have happened to change your attitude." She chuckled. "You don't have to be Sherlock Holmes to figure out that one."

"About yesterday," Sarah began, when Aunt Pam held up her hand.

"Not a word," she said, her eyes warm with affection. "I know it was a shock, and you reacted the way anyone would. But now," she said briskly, "I can sense that you've come to accept it a little better, haven't you? And I think you realize that I'm always going to be here for you, to help you, and to answer your questions." She peered at Sarah across the table. "You look much calmer — happier — today."

For the next ten minutes, Sarah told her everything about the dance, the costumes, and the strange incident with the grape punch. "Honestly, Aunt Pam," she said, "I didn't wish for the punch to spill over Allison." She frowned. "At least, I don't think I did. I was staring at the glass and it just tipped over."

"This is just the beginning, you know," Aunt Pam told her. "Now," she said, getting up to refill the teapot, "I bet there are questions you want to ask me."

Chapter 7

An hour later, the midmorning sunlight inched its way across the butcher-block table, picking up the flecks of copper in Aunt Pam's raven hair. Sarah was leaning forward eagerly, asking every question about being a witch she could think of. There was so much to learn! And according to her aunt, experience was the best teacher. Most of what she would learn would come from trial and error.

"I don't even know where to start," Sarah said, her dark eyes glowing. "I wish I had known about all this years ago," she sighed.

"Why's that?"

Sarah chuckled. "Well, you're going to think this is silly, but there was an awful kid in third grade called Danny Gleason. He sat right behind me in homeroom, and he used to pull my pigtails, and then laugh like a hyena. I got so mad, I used to wish I could wave a magic wand and turn him *into* a hyena."

Aunt Pam shook her head. "A tempting idea, but it would never work — even if you had known earlier. Witches can't alter human structure. There's no way you could turn a boy into a hyena."

"Really?" Sarah looked disappointed. "How about a frog?"

"Sorry. *That* myth has been going around for a long time."

"Oh." Sarah was silent for a moment, thinking. The sunlight snaking across the table reminded her of a sundial, and she said suddenly, "Can I change what time it is? That way I could add extra time onto the weekends!" She was ecstatic at the idea, but Aunt Pam dashed her hopes.

" 'Fraid not. Of course, you can try it, if you like." Aunt Pam was watching her carefully. She tapped her long fingernails on the edge of her saucer, and smiled tolerantly. "That way, you'll know for sure."

Sarah licked her lips nervously. "I'll give it a try." She looked at the black cat clock with the darting eyes and twitching tail that hung over the sofa. "It's almost ten," she said, focusing all her attention on the clock, "but when I open my eyes, it will be . . . nine o'clock!" Using every ounce of energy in her body, Sarah squeezed her eyes tightly shut and concentrated hard. When she opened them, she was astounded.

The clock had rolled back an hour. It was now nine o'clock!

"I thought you said it didn't work," Sarah said reproachfully.

Aunt Pam looked at her watch and held up her hand for silence. "Six, five, four, three, two, one . . . there it goes." As she dropped her hand, she turned to the open window and Sarah followed her gaze. Immediately, the loud pealing of a church bell drifted through the window, and Sarah started counting.

When the bell stopped, Sarah frowned. "That doesn't make sense. The bell rang ten times."

"It's ten o'clock," Aunt Pam said patiently.

"But the clock — " Sarah interrupted.

"The clock's wrong," her aunt said firmly. "You managed to change the hands on the clock, but you didn't change time. There's a big difference."

"Oh," Sarah said, feeling a little crushed. "I see what you mean."

"It will all start making sense to you," Aunt Pam promised. She snapped her fingers, and the small hand on the cat clock inched forward to ten.

"Wow — you did that so quickly! Don't you have to close your eyes and concentrate?" Sarah asked, impressed.

"Not anymore."

Sarah pushed her hair out of her eyes, wondering if she would ever get it all straight. At the moment, she felt completely confused.

As always, Aunt Pam seemed to read her thoughts, and said sympathetically, "Don't try to absorb it all at once. Give yourself some time."

"Oh, I will," Sarah said vaguely. She had no intention of sitting around trying to figure it out. She was dying to get home and start practicing. Okay, so she couldn't change time, and she couldn't change people into frogs, but there must be dozens of other exciting things she *could* do!

"The details don't really matter," her aunt was saying earnestly. "The important thing to remember is that you have a power, and a lot of responsibility goes along with it."

"Oh, sure, I know that," Sarah said. She tried to look interested, but she fidgeted a little, wondering when she could politely make her getaway.

"I hope you really mean that," Aunt Pam added. "The key to being a good witch is learning when to use your powers . . . and how. If they are used wrongly, or unwisely, they're sure to backfire."

"Right," Sarah said, scraping back her chair. She was glad she'd had a chance to ask about specifics, like the frog and the clock, but the last thing she wanted was a little lecture on responsibility. Aunt Pam was beginning to sound just a tiny bit like her homeroom teacher!

"Remember, Sarah. It's up to you to make the right choices." A frown flitted across her aunt's perfect features, and Sarah wondered guiltily if she knew what she was thinking.

"I will," Sarah assured her. "You can count on it."

Her aunt enveloped her in a hug at the door. "I hope so, Sarah. Come back soon, and we'll talk some more. And be sure to call me anytime you have a question."

Sarah practically floated up the front steps of her house, still thinking about her conversation with Aunt Pam. She felt as if a whole new world had been opened to her. Being a witch could be a wonderful thing, she was convinced of that now, and it would be fun to investigate all the exciting possibilities. It could certainly help her with grades, and friends, and boys. Boys! She suddenly thought of Cody Rice. Maybe she could use her powers to make him notice her. She'd have to check that out right away. Maybe there was a certain perfume she could wear, or a certain color, and he'd take one look and say. . . .

"It's not your lucky day!"

Startled, Sarah yanked her thoughts back to the real world as her brother met her at the front door. He was wearing a sly grin and a chef's apron; his hands were covered with flour.

"Why not?" she asked wearily, knowing what was coming.

"Because Dad and I fixed pancakes, and guess what?" Simon chortled loudly. "It's *your* day for the kitchen!" He tore the apron off and reached for his windbreaker.

"Oh, no," Sarah groaned. Everyone took turns with the household chores, and the official "switch day," when everyone switched jobs, was Sunday.

She walked into the kitchen, expecting the worst. She found it.

"Hi, honey!" Dr. Connell said cheerfully. "Hope you're hungry; we made enough to feed an army."

"I can see that," Sarah said, her spirits sinking fast. The kitchen was a complete disaster!

"We went all-out," her father added, sounding pleased. "I was going to stop with pancakes. But Simon suggested we make wheat germ muffins, since we already had the batter made," he explained, waving a floury hand toward a stack of stainless steel mixing bowls.

"How thoughtful of him," Sarah muttered. Simon always seemed to get insane food cravings when it was *her* day for the kitchen! When it was *his* day, he popped a bunch of frozen waffles in the toaster and plunked a bottle of maple syrup on the table.

"I'd love to help you, but — " he stopped as a buzzer sounded in the kitchen. Three longs and two shorts. "Duty calls," he finished, whipping off his apron. "Emma came in today so we could catch up on the paperwork."

"That's okay," Sarah said resignedly. The buzzer was a signal that Emma, Dr. Connell's receptionist, had worked out to let him know that he was needed.

"Mom had some errands to run, but maybe Nicole went out, I think," he said vaguely. His mind was already on his work. When he reached the connecting door, he stopped and gave Sarah a dazzling smile. "Hey, I want to hear all about your dance last night," he said hurriedly. "Put me on your schedule for later."

"I will." Sarah grinned at him, pleased. No matter how busy her father was, he always made time for her.

When he disappeared into his office suite, Sarah took stock of the situation. Her eyes did a slow pan over the cluttered counter, sticky table, and overflowing sink. Dad and Simon must have used every pot and pan in the house! And neatness was never one of Dad's strong points, she thought, grimacing as she stepped into a puddle of pancake batter on the floor. "Ugh!" she muttered. "I've got better things to do with my time than this."

She started to put the kettle on for a cup of tea and suddenly paused, thinking. Could a witch clean up a kitchen? The idea was exciting. Would it work? Could she just wish the whole mess away? Maybe! This was the perfect time to test her powers. Neither her mother nor Nicole would be back for hours, so she'd have the whole place to herself. No one would ever know. They'd think she'd been working her fingers to the bone!

"Well . . . in that case," she said slowly, "I'll start with a little experiment. Let's make some tea." She sat down at the kitchen table and put her feet on the arm of the adjacent chair. This was the life! It was going to be fun to be waited on.

Now came the tough part. Where to start? "Hmmm," she said thoughtfully. "I guess the first thing I need is a cup." She stared hard at the cupboard, wishing that a cup would magically appear in her hand. Nothing happened for a minute, and then she shook her head annoyed.

"What an idiot!" she said aloud. "I forgot to shut my eyes." She tilted her head back and squeezed her eyes closed. "Cup . . . appear," she said firmly. She wasn't sure if she was supposed to say anything, but she had seen a magician do that once on a TV show, and it had worked.

She was startled to hear a dull thump against the cupboard door. "What in the world — " she cried.

She had forgotten to open the cupboard door! The cup was trapped inside, batting itself against the sturdy oak cabinet.

"Wait, stop that!" she yelled, scrambling to her feet. She dashed to the cupboard and flung open the door. The cup dropped lightly into her hand, and she breathed a sigh of relief. Another few thumps, and the stoneware cup would have been smashed to bits.

She was trying to decide what to do next, when her mother's voice made her jump.

"Who were you talking to?" her mother asked curiously. She dropped an armful of groceries on the kitchen table and looked around in dismay. "Uh-oh," she said dejectedly. "Looks like Dad and Simon were at it again."

"You're right," Sarah said, glad to change the subject. "But I'll have this all cleaned up in a jiffy," she offered. "It will only take a minute, honest. I'll just get a clean cloth, and start with the table — " She knew that she was talking much too fast — the way she always did when she was nervous — and her mother was giving her a strange look.

"Sarah, are you all right?"

"All right?" Sarah babbled, rushing to clean the table. "Of course I'm all right. Why wouldn't I be all right?"

Her mother raised a skeptical eyebrow. "Well, you seem a little hyper, for one thing, and I was sure I heard you talking to someone a few minutes ago."

"Talking to someone? No, that was just the

radio." Sarah ducked her head and started dabbing vigorously at an orange juice stain in the middle of the table. "I was listening to the radio."

Her mother frowned. "Sarah, the radio isn't turned on."

Sarah froze as her mother stared at the little pink portable radio Sarah had been given for her birthday. Sarah shut her eyes and wished furiously. *Radio — on!* she said silently.

Just as her mother reached for the radio, it sprang to life. She darted back in surprise, as a heavy metal song filled the room. "Guess I was wrong," she said, still puzzled.

"They were off the air for a few minutes," Sarah said, improvising wildly. "It was one of those emergency tests."

"Oh," her mother said, tackling the groceries. "How was the dance last night?"

"It was great," Sarah said, watching in dismay as her mother started methodically cleaning out the fridge. From the looks of things, her mother was going to spend the rest of the morning in the kitchen. Sarah took another look at the disaster waiting on every counter. She wouldn't be able to use any of her magic on the kitchen this time. She reached for a dish cloth and began scrubbing the sticky countertop. Think positively, she told herself. There would be plenty of other times to test her powers.

"Why'd you leave my house so early?" Micki demanded a couple of hours later. She had dropped in to see Sarah, who had just finished the kitchen, and was munching on a giant peanut butter sandwich. "I . . . uh . . . wanted to see my Aunt Pam," Sarah said. "I hope I didn't wake you up."

"No, you didn't," Micki confessed, sliding into a seat at the round oak table. "I just fell out of bed a few minutes ago." She nibbled on a cracker and looked happily around the kitchen. "I love your house on the weekends," she said. "There's always so much going on."

"That's for sure," Sarah muttered. The kitchen was a madhouse. Dr. Connell had finished his morning work and was busily concocting a banana milk shake in the blender; her mother was chatting with a school counselor on the phone; and Simon was dribbling a basketball near the sink. Only Nicole remained aloof. She was reading a paperback and had insulated herself from the noise by wearing a pair of headphones.

"I was on my way to the library, and I wondered if you'd like to come with me," Micki suggested.

"The library?"

Micki made a face. "In case you've forgotten, we've got a history term paper due in a couple of weeks."

"I *had* forgotten," Sarah said, polishing off the last of her juice. "Two weeks," she said lazily. "What's the rush? We've got plenty of time. I haven't even picked a topic yet."

"Neither have I. I can't decide if I should do my paper on the French Revolution or on the building of the Pyramids," Micki said. "Oh, well, I guess the library has books on everything."

Sarah let her mind wander as Micki rambled on. "Books on everything," she repeated softly. Of course! She could probably find out a lot of information on witches in the library! Why hadn't she thought about it before? Aunt Pam was still the expert, of course, but it would be nice to do a little "independent research," as her English teacher said.

Sarah swallowed the last bite of her sandwich and jumped to her feet. "Hurry up, Micki," she said, pulling her friend out of the chair. "The library closes early on Sunday, and we're wasting time!"

Micki looked surprised. "I thought you said there was no rush."

"I was wrong!" Sarah said excitedly. "I want to get started now. Right this minute!"

Micki shook her head. "You certainly are acting strange, Sarah." She grabbed her jacket as Sarah propelled her down the front hall.

Chapter 8

"I'm looking for something on witches," Sarah whispered half an hour later to Mrs. Gibbs, the reference librarian at the Waterview Public Library. "It's for a term paper."

She glanced nervously at the winding stairway that led to the second floor. Micki had dashed upstairs to find a book on King Tut, and Sarah fervently hoped she'd be gone for more than a few minutes. How could she ever explain her sudden interest in witches to her friend?

"I see," Mrs. Gibbs said, reaching for a notepad. "Modern or medieval witches?" she asked crisply.

Sarah's mind stalled. "Uh . . . modern, I guess. But maybe I better look into the medieval ones, too. My teacher would probably like that," she added quickly.

"It's always wise to consider the historical perspective." The librarian nodded approvingly. "Now the next question is, are you including warlocks in your paper or limiting it to witches?"

"Warlocks?" Sarah said blankly.

"Warlocks are male witches."

"Oh, no," she said quickly. "Just . . . female witches. That's all I'm interested in."

"Eastern or western hemisphere?"

"Uh, western. I guess."

Sarah waited in an agony of suspense while Mrs. Gibbs slowly flipped through a card catalogue. She took another quick peek at the stairway. There was no sign of Micki. So far, so good.

"Central European, Northern European, or American?"

"Uh . . . American, I think," Sarah stammered. This was worse than Baskin-Robbins! Who would have guessed this would be so complicated?

"Pre-Salem or post-Salem?"

"What?"

"The Salem Witch Trials," Mrs. Gibbs said, tapping her pencil against a steno pad. "They were in 1692."

"Yes, we studied about that," Sarah said, happy to find something she recognized. "I guess . . . I'm more interested in witches *after* Salem," she decided. She could always go back and read about the early history of witches when she had more time.

She hopped from one foot to another while Mrs. Gibbs scribbled down a series of numbers, and then handed her a long sheet of paper. "This should keep you busy for a while," she told her. "And we can always get more books on interlibrary loan."

Sarah looked at the list in dismay. Interlibrary loan! It would take her weeks just to wade through these.

"Any luck?" Micki said brightly. She had come up silently behind her.

"Oh, yes, they have tons of stuff here," Sarah answered. She crunched up the list into a tight ball and tried to jam it into her pocket. "How are you doing?"

"I think I'll concentrate on Egyptian art. What's your topic?" Micki said, eyeing the piece of paper with interest.

"Ummm . . . probably fashion styles in the eighteenth century."

Micki wrinkled her nose. "Sounds like it will take a lot of research," she commented.

"Oh, it will," Sarah agreed, eager to get started.

"But at least it's something you're really interested in," Micki said. When she saw the startled look on Sarah's face, she added, "Since you want to be a fashion designer, I mean."

"Oh, yes, you're right," Sarah said quickly. "This is something I'm *very* interested in."

Luckily, Micki decided to study on the mezzanine, since most of the art history books she needed were too heavy to lug downstairs, and Sarah could work undisturbed. She spent the next two hours writing frantically in her looseleaf notebook, stopping occasionally to lean back and stretch. There was so much to read and discover, she thought.

She felt a little tingle of excitement when she read that witches possessed amazing powers. They could find lost objects, foretell the future, and fly through the air. Some people even said that witches could make themselves invisible.

"Wouldn't *that* be something!" she muttered under her breath. The possibilities were endless — being a witch was going to be even more far out than she had imagined.

Sarah chuckled softly to herself. Wow, she thought, shaking her head.

"What's so funny?" Micki said, interrupting her thoughts. She slid into the seat next to her, her curly red hair damp on her forehead.

"Oh, just the weird styles they used to wear," Sarah said, hastily shutting the book. "How come your face is so red?" she said, changing the subject. "You look like you've been running a marathon."

"It's like a sauna upstairs," Micki said, grimacing. She glanced at her watch. "Hey! Do you realize we've been slaving over this stuff for two hours! How about grabbing a hamburger?"

"Sounds good to me," Sarah said, standing up quickly. "Let's go to Carmichael's."

Micki frowned. "Shouldn't we put your books back on the shelves?" Her hand was resting lightly on top of an old volume called *The History of Witches* but luckily the title was so faded it was impossible to read.

"No," Sarah said quickly. "The librarians like to file them back themselves. That way they make sure they get back in the right place." She felt a little pang of guilt when Micki gave her a trusting smile and dropped the book on the table. She hated to lie to her best friend, but right now she had no other choice.

Carmichael's was jammed when Micki and Sarah gave their order to a harried-looking waitress a few minutes later.

"It looks like *everyone* is here today," Micki said, glancing around the busy restaurant. Carmichael's was a cheerful place with butcher-block tables and Tiffany lamps, which was popular with the Waterview High students. "Look, there's Heather Larson and Tina Jordan." She jumped up and gave a loud whistle, and the two girls smiled and headed toward their table.

"I was wondering if we were going to find a seat," Heather said, squeezing into the red leather booth next to Micki.

"Look," Micki suddenly said. "There's your cowboy." She looked toward the salad bar.

"Your cowboy?" Tina asked, arching a dark eyebrow.

Sarah flushed. "Micki's kidding," she said, making a face at her friend. "I met a new boy at school — Cody Rice — and since he dresses like he's from the West, Micki calls him a cowboy."

"He's cute," Heather said promptly.

"Ohmigosh," Sarah said, turning and catching a glimpse of Cody. "That's him, all right."

Micki laughed at her serious expression, and

said teasingly, "Love at first sight. Or actually, second sight. Sarah met him at the hot chocolate machine one morning."

"How did you remember that?" Sarah asked in surprise.

Micki's eyes twinkled. "Well, I remember you had a chocolate mustache all during homeroom and first period."

"No!" Sarah wailed. "I'll die." She put her head in her hands, and then peeked out between her fingers. "How can I ever face him again?"

"Maybe he won't remember," Heather said helpfully.

"He won't remember meeting her?" Tina objected. "That's not very flattering."

"No, I mean maybe he'll remember meeting her, but he'll forget about the mustache."

Sarah ignored her giggling friends, and focused all her attention on Cody. Had she really looked like an idiot the first time she had met him? A chocolate mustache! How embarrassing. No wonder he had wanted to get away as fast as he could. She would never drink hot chocolate again. She had probably made a terrible first impression on him. . . . The point was, what could she do about it now?

Sarah stood up slowly. She wanted to see Cody Rice, and she knew it was now or never. "I've got this sudden craving for a salad."

The first thing to do, she decided, as she reached for a plate, was to make him totally forget their first meeting. And especially the chocolate mustache. She hovered behind a lettuce bowl the size of a laundry basket, and pretended to scan the salad bar.

Squeezing her eyes tightly shut, she concentrated as hard as she could. Let him forget about the mustache, she said silently. She repeated it twice, just to make sure, and when she opened her eyes, she decided to take another peek at Cody.

He was sitting by himself at a small table by the window, his dark hair flecked with gold in the bright sunlight. He looked even more handsome than the day she had met him, and his eyes were startlingly blue against his lightly tanned skin.

She could have stared at him forever, but someone nudged her elbow and she reached for a fork and napkin. She began filling her plate randomly, making her way slowly down the aisle to where Cody was sitting. She knew that when she reached the end of the table, where the salad dressings were arranged in metal tubs, she could "accidentally" spot him and say hello.

She rounded the corner and helped herself to blue cheese dressing. Squaring her shoulders, she took a deep breath and said brightly, "Hi there."

Cody looked up, his impossibly blue eyes flickering over her. "Hi," he said slowly, and she waited for recognition to flood his face. He was wearing an off-white shaker-knit sweater with a pair of faded jeans, and he looked terrific.

"We met in the teacher's lounge. The first day of school," she prompted him.

"Of course," he said, snapping his fingers. "You're. . . ."

"Sarah Connell." She balanced her tray awkwardly, wishing he would ask her to sit down. In a few more seconds, the people in line behind her would catch up with her, and it would be embarrassing. She ducked to the side as a waitress scurried by with a tray.

"I'm Cody Rice," he said pleasantly.

"Of course you are," she blurted out, and felt like biting off her tongue. What a dumb thing to say! He started to smile, and she could feel herself getting red up to her hairline. "I mean,

I remember you," she stammered.

"That's very nice of you," he said sincerely. He rested his chin in his hand and looked thoughtful. "It's the funniest thing, but there was something different about you. That day in the teacher's lounge, I mean. . . ."

"Oh, really?" Sarah said, giggling foolishly. The mustache! Darn it — she must not have erased the memory of it completely. "I can't imagine what it could be." She shifted uncomfortably from one foot to the other. Was he never going to ask her to sit down?

"I'll get it in a minute," he assured her. "I never forget a pretty girl." He stared at her for a long moment, and Sarah wished she could sink into the floor. Then his face lit up, just like someone had turned on a light bulb over his head. "That's it!" he said suddenly. "There was something different about your face." He leaned forward eagerly, his hamburger forgotten. "Not your eyes, not your nose. . . ." He frowned, squinting at her mouth.

Before he could say another word, Sarah stood stock-still and closed her eyes. *Let him forget about the teacher's lounge!* she wished frantically. She didn't bother repeating the wish but tried to put ever ounce of energy into her words.

Fearfully, she opened her eyes to see Cody calmly taking a bite of hamburger. It had worked! She was so new at this witch business, she was never quite sure how any of her wishes would actually turn out.

She edged a little closer to his table, and her napkin fluttered off her tray. Cody bent down to retrieve it, and handed it to her absently.

"Here you are," he said in a casual tone, returning to his hamburger, as if she were a total stranger.

"Cody?" Sarah said, puzzled.

Cody looked up, startled. "Yes, that's right," he said agreeably. He stared blankly at her and Sarah felt the color drain right out of her face.

"Don't you . . . know who I am?" she gasped.

And then he said the words that shook her all the way down to her socks.

"No," he said politely. "Should I?"

No? What was going on? She must have done something terribly wrong.

He stood up slowly and stuck out his hand. "I'm Cody Rice. . . ." His voice was flat and expressionless, as if he were talking to a tree. He had absolutely no idea in the world who she was. She had really blown it this time, she thought miserably. She had accidentally erased all memory of their meeting!

"I'm sorry, it's my mistake," Sarah blurted out. "I . . . uh, thought you were someone else."

"Hey, it's okay. No harm done."

No harm done! Cody was waiting politely for her to leave, probably dying to get back to his hamburger. Now what? Sarah shifted uncomfortably, trying to think of something to say. "Well, uh, it was nice meeting you," she said lamely.

"Yeah, you, too." He sat down and reached for his napkin, not giving her another thought.

Nothing was working out like she had planned! She had certainly done something wrong to make him totally forget her. This witch business wasn't going to be easy!

Chapter 9

"Are you okay? You look a little pale," Micki said a few minutes later. Sarah had rejoined her friends, trying to make sense out of what had just happened.

Cody had forgotten her. Just like that! It was amazing, and a little scary to think what she had accomplished with her magic powers. She had simply wished that he would forget all about the chocolate mustache and her wish had come true! Except she had gotten more than she bargained for. Cody had forgotten that she even existed.

"I'm fine," Sarah said a little uncertainly. She realized that everyone was staring at her, and she decided she had better act casual. "I just felt a little dizzy when I was standing at the salad bar."

"I know what you mean," Heather piped up.

"Remember last semester when I tried a vegetarian diet? I ate so many celery stalks, I caught myself leaning toward the sun!"

Later, when they were walking home together, Micki said, "Sarah, *what* was going on in Carmichael's?"

"Nothing," Sarah said. She gave Micki a reassuring squeeze on the arm, and added, "I guess I'm just a little uptight about my term paper. I think I let it go too long this time."

At home, she poured a glass of milk and helped Simon empty the dishwasher, feeling at loose ends. There were so many unanswered questions. What about the incident at Carmichael's that day? It looked like being a witch wasn't a very exact science, at least not the way she was practicing it, she thought ruefully. She was shocked to think that she had erased a big chunk of Cody's memory. What if she started making other, more serious mistakes? It was scary to think what could happen. She knew that there was only one person who could help her — her aunt.

"Now what is it that has you so confused?" Aunt Pam said half an hour later. She reached over and brushed Sarah's brown hair out of her eyes, her delicate gold bracelets clinking together on her arm. They were alone in Plates and Pages, and the late afternoon sunlight streamed in the front windows, bouncing off the rows of brightly bound books.

Sarah shrugged, wondering where to start. "There's just so much to figure out, so much to learn," she said, shaking her head.

"Well, you didn't think you'd master everything just like that, did you? In one day?" Aunt Pam snapped her fingers in the air and gave a musical little laugh.

"I guess not."

"Of course not!" Aunt Pam said warmly. She peered at Sarah, cupping her chin in her hand. "You didn't learn English and history just like that, did you? And you certainly didn't pick up algebra in a snap. You had to start by learning the multiplication tables."

Sarah nodded. "I guess I thought that since this was magic . . . it would be easy. Whenever anyone does a magic trick on TV, it always turns out just the way they want it to."

Sarah told her about the library books she had read, and her aunt smiled. "You should have come to me first," she said sliding off her stool at the cash register as a customer came in. "I've got tons of books you can borrow." She pointed toward the back of the shop. "Start with that bottom shelf on the far wall." She smiled. "That should keep you busy while I help Mrs. Davis with her mystery books."

A few minutes later, Sarah settled down cross-legged in a narrow aisle. There were dozens of books to choose from, but a small volume with a faded yellow cover caught her eye. It was about the size of a diary, and when she opened it, she was surprised to find that the pages were lined, and the book was filled with elegant handwriting in violet ink.

"*Spells and Potions*," she said softly. "How super!" This was exactly what she needed, she decided, thumbing through the pages. "How to fly, how to change your appearance, how to change your voice. . . ." There were spells for all sorts of situations, but Sarah thought some of them sounded a bit tricky, and she wasn't sure she should attempt them. "How to become invisible," she read. "Warning: This spell is reserved for advanced witches only."

"Darn," she muttered. "Maybe I'd better start with something simpler." She turned to the index and read: *Potions: Love*.

"That's it!" she cried excitedly. "Love potions!" She nearly scrambled to her feet to ask

Aunt Pam about them, but she noticed just in time that her aunt was still busy with Mrs. Davis, and she reluctantly settled back down. She'd just have to figure this out for herself.

When her aunt finally joined her ten minutes later, Sarah had carefully copied down the recipe for a love potion that was "guaranteed to ignite the flames of love in any red-blooded male." She smiled at the corny phrase.

"The flames of love," Sarah said softly. "Not bad!"

"The spells and potions books are fun, aren't they?" Aunt Pam said, joining her on the floor. "That yellow one you're holding is over a hundred years old."

"Really?" Sarah said, running her hand over the fine leather. "It has exactly what I need."

"It does?" Aunt Pam looked surprised, and Sarah quickly told her about the episode with Cody Rice, and her plans for him. "Oh, no," her aunt groaned. "Sarah, I gave you the books because I thought you'd enjoy reading them. You can't start experimenting with ancient recipes."

"Well, why shouldn't I try a few?" Sarah said defensively. "The spells and potions work, don't they?"

"Sometimes," Aunt Pam admitted. "But not

always." Sarah started to interrupt her and she held up her hand. "You'd be surprised at how much can go wrong, especially in the hands of an inexperienced witch. Remember what you just told me about Cody Rice? You not only wished away the mustache, you wished away all memory of you!"

"That was an accident," Sarah said plaintively. "I'll be more careful the next time, honest!"

"It's not a question of being careful," Aunt Pam said. "It takes years of — oh, darn!" She broke off suddenly as a portly man with a briefcase entered the shop. "That's Professor Watlington. I promised I'd help him with some research," she whispered.

"That's okay," Sarah said quickly. "I have to be running along anyway." She shoved the book in her pocket and walked quickly down the aisle before Aunt Pam could object. The next hour would be the most important one of her whole life, she thought. She had already decided that the moment she got home, she was going to whip up a sure-fire magic potion that would make Cody Rice fall hopelessly, desperately, in love with her!

Unfortunately Sarah had to wait until much later that night to begin work on the potion.

After dinner, Nicole decided to make a batch of chocolate chip cookies, and Simon had had a sudden craving for popcorn. It was nearly ten-thirty when Sarah finally found herself alone in the kitchen, and she quietly shut the door that led to the den.

"It's just you and me," she said to Bandit, who was dozing by the fridge. "Although I'm not sure how much help you'll be," she said wryly.

She spread her notes out on the counter and started pulling ingredients out of the kitchen cabinets. Luckily she could find most of the things she needed on the top shelf of the pantry — herbs and spices with funny-sounding names like turmeric, cumin, and marjoram. She wondered what the concoction would taste like.

Then she hit a snag. The potion called for all sorts of weird plants! "Hibiscus flowers, rose petals, lemon grass, and ginger root," she read. She had no idea where to get those things. She started tearing the cupboards apart, wondering if she could improvise, when she came across her mother's gourmet tea collection. There was a box labeled "Cherry Blossom Special," which smelled exactly like cough syrup, and had almost everything she needed in it.

Another box, "Orange Delight," contained ginger root powder. "That's close enough!" Sarah said. She began cooking a sticky mixture of something that looked like black tar, when Nicole stuck her head in the door.

"Wow, what stinks?" she asked loudly. Sarah rushed to close the door leading to the den. All she needed was to have the rest of the family come trooping in!

"Nothing," Sarah told her. "I just felt like a snack."

Nicole gingerly lifted the lid on the pan and made a face. "Ugh. You decided to cook curry at this time of the night?"

"Is that what it is — curry?" Sarah asked, surprised.

Nicole gave her a puzzled look. "It smells like curry to me," she explained. "Don't you even know what you're cooking?"

Sarah was trying to think of a clever retort when Simon barged into the kitchen. Oh, no, she thought, her spirits sinking. This was all she needed.

"Hey, what smells good?" he asked, sniffing around the stove.

"I'm cooking some spices . . . for curry," Sarah said, trying to sound as convincing as she could.

"Can I sprinkle some on my popcorn?" he said hopefully.

"You are really gross!" Nicole told him, and he laughed.

"There's not enough to go around," Sarah said, slapping his hand as he reached for the blackened pan. By this time the whole kitchen smelled like someone was cooking old inner tubes, and Sarah held her breath, afraid her parents would appear at any minute.

It was another ten minutes before Sarah got Nicole and Simon out of the kitchen. By the time she had finished making the potion, the final product was a grainy powder the color of egg yolks. It had a gritty feel to it, and when she touched the spoon to her tongue, it left a strange metallic aftertaste. No one in their right mind would touch it.

I've got to add something to it, she thought. Taking a wild chance, she dumped a cup of sugar into the pan. She sniffed it tentatively. Not bad . . . Then she scooped the mixture into a plastic container and sealed it tightly shut.

There must be some way to get Cody Rice to eat it! She decided to hide the potion in the bottom of her locker for safekeeping. Maybe she'd have an inspiration in the next few days.

* * *

It was Micki who provided her with the perfect opportunity the very next day. The dismissal bell had just rung and Sarah was stashing her notebooks in her battered green locker when Micki ran up to her.

"Do me a big favor?" Micki asked breathlessly. Her face was flushed, and she was holding a stack of paper cups.

"Sure, what's up?"

Micki smiled gratefully and handed her a cigar box. "Come out to football practice with me. We're selling lemonade to make money for new band uniforms."

"You want me to sell lemonade?" Sarah sighed. "I don't know. . . ." Trudging around a dusty football field didn't seem like a fun way to spend the afternoon.

"Please!" Micki said urgently. "I can't pour and keep track of the money at the same time."

"All right, all right," Sarah agreed. "Go ahead. I'll be there in a minute." She slammed the locker door shut and started to twirl the combination lock when a thought struck her. Maybe . . . just *maybe* Cody Rice would be there, and if he decided to buy a lemonade. . . . Her heart thumping, she quickly opened her locker and reached for the plastic container.

* * *

"It's pretty hot, so I bet we'll have lots of customers today," Micki said a few minutes later, scanning the bleachers. She had set up glass pitchers of lemonade on a card table at the edge of the playing field, and started pouring as a few kids made their way toward her.

Sarah was doing her best to remain calm, but her heart was doing a drumbeat in her chest, and she couldn't resist checking out the bleachers for Cody. She had almost given up, when a thatch of gleaming blue-black hair caught her eye. No one but Cody Rice had hair like that!

Now that she had spotted Cody, all she had to do was make him buy a lemonade! She had transferred some of the potion to a plastic sandwich bag left over from lunch, and she fingered it nervously in her pocket. She wasn't sure how she would handle the actual transfer. She'd worry about that when the time came.

A line started forming in front of the lemonade stand, and she started making change in the cigar box as Micki filled the paper cups. She caught sight of Cody looking over, and without thinking, she squeezed her eyes shut and made a wish.

Buy a lemonade, Cody, she said silently,

willing him to approach the table. When she opened her eyes, he was crossing the field, heading right toward them!

Micki spotted him at the same time, and she said under her breath, "Oh, look, there's that guy you like."

Sarah ignored her, and shoved her right hand in her pocket. She had no idea how she was going to get the potion in his drink! Before she could give it another thought, he was standing in front of her.

"One lemonade," he said politely.

"Coming up," Micki answered, her eyes flickering to Sarah.

"That will be a quarter," Sarah said, her heart pounding. Her hand was so damp, it was sticking to the plastic bag.

"Here you go," Cody said, tossing some change in the cigar box. He reached for the paper cup, but Sarah was too quick for him.

"Would you care for sweetened or unsweetened lemonade?" she said in a sudden burst of inspiration. When he hesitated, she added quickly, "The unsweetened is pretty bitter. It's like eating a sour lemon."

"Oh, well, sweetened then," he said.

She knew Micki was straining to hear every

word, but the band started practicing just then, and the bass drums drowned out her words.

In one swift movement, she yanked the sandwich bag out of her pocket, and emptied it in the paper cup before Cody's startled eyes. She stirred the mixture quickly with a plastic spoon and handed it to him.

"That's funny-looking sugar," he said suspiciously.

"It's natural brown sugar," she told him, innocently. "It's much healthier than white sugar." She paused. "My father's a doctor, you know."

"Oh," he said, nodding. "Well, thanks very much." He smiled and moved off.

The minute he was gone, Micki leaned over and hissed, "What was all that about sweetened and unsweetened? You know darn well this stuff comes from a mix. It's probably ninety-percent sugar anyway!"

"Really? Well, I didn't want to say anything, but that last batch was really bad. I tried some while you were setting up the table."

Micki frowned and peered at the empty pitcher. "Well, this one's finished," she said, reaching under the card table. "I'll be more careful mixing the next batch."

Chapter 10

The only thing to do now was wait, Sarah told herself later that evening. It was nearly eight-thirty, and she figured that Cody had taken the lemonade with the love potion four hours ago. She wondered when it would take effect, but decided against calling Aunt Pam, who might give her a lecture on "responsibility."

She was propped up in bed, dividing her time between her French homework and an old *Monkees* rerun when the phone rang. It must be Micki, she decided. She always had trouble with irregular French verbs, too.

It was Cody.

"I've got to talk to you," he said in that husky drawl that sent shivers all the way down to her toes. *I've got to talk to you.* Just like that.

"How did you get my phone number?" Not

the most romantic thing in the world to say, but she was curious.

He laughed. "How many David Connells, M.D., could there be in the Waterview phone book?"

Of course. She had told him her father was a doctor when he'd bought the lemonade. She was wondering what to say next, when he gave her another shock.

" 'How do I love thee? Let me count the ways. . . .' "

Ohmigosh! He was quoting *love* poetry to her! She recognized the line from Elizabeth Barrett Browning; they were studying her poems in Mr. Ferris's class. The love potion had really *worked*! She could hardly believe it.

Cody paused after a few verses, waiting for a reply, and for the life of her, she couldn't think of a thing to say.

"That's . . . that's very nice," she said finally.

"It can't begin to describe what I *really* feel for you," he said, his voice low and sincere.

Another long pause. "Oh." Sarah had never been so tongue-tied in her life. What were you supposed to do when a boy declared undying love? Were you supposed to act surprised, or should you tell him that you love him, too? Why hadn't she thought of all this earlier! Her mind was a blank, and she was gripping the phone so tightly, her knuckles had turned white. She was handling this terribly. At the rate she was going, Cody would think she was the most boring girl he had ever met. Surprisingly though, he didn't seem the least bit put off by her silence.

After a moment, he said softly, "I'd like to see you tomorrow."

"I . . . well, I guess — "

"We can make it after school, if you're busy in the evening."

He thought she was stalling, that maybe she didn't want to go out with him. She decided she'd better find her voice — fast!

"After school is fine," she said quickly. "What did you have in mind?"

"Carmichael's," he answered, sounding surprised. "After all, that's where we met."

"Oh, yes, of course," she babbled. He *had* forgotten all about that day in the teacher's lounge.

"I'll see you there at three-thirty," he said, his voice warm and affectionate. "That's just nineteen hours away," he added wistfully. "I'll be counting the minutes."

"Right," Sarah said. The love potion had fulfilled her wildest expectations. Who would ever *think* he would fall in love with her so quickly, or so completely? She supposed that her whole life would change now that she had Cody. Would he call her every night? she wondered. Would he see her every weekend? He was in the middle of another love poem when Sarah glanced at the clock. She had been on the phone for fifteen minutes, and Cody gave no signs of slowing down.

Regretfully, Sarah finally cut him off by saying that her father needed to use the phone. She blushed furiously while he treated her to a long, heartfelt good-bye.

"Good-night, my love, till we meet tomorrow."

Finally she managed to hang up. Then she sat straight up in bed, staring blankly at the mirror.

"Who would ever think I could have that effect on a boy?" she said out loud. Of course, it was all due to her love potion, she admitted ruefully. Cody had acted like she was invisible that afternoon at Carmichael's, and it was obvious that without the potion, he'd never have given her a second glance. Still, what was she complaining about? She must be doing *something* right. Cody was madly in love with her!

* * *

She woke up the next morning in an agony of indecision. This would be a day she would remember forever. What should she wear? She rummaged wildly through her closet, wishing for once that she was more organized. There were dozens of possibilities, but all her clothes were crunched together so tightly, it was hard to see what was there. She glanced at her bulletin board for inspiration, as she always did when she was stumped, and spotted an outfit she had cut out of *Seventeen*.

The model was about her height and had curly brown hair and dark eyes. She was wearing one of those lace-collared sweaters with a pair of jeans and tight-fitting brown leather boots. The outfit was simple, and yet it looked just right for a fall day.

Sarah had bought a bright yellow sweater, very similar to the one in the magazine, and she yanked it out of her drawer. She pulled it over her head and reached for her favorite ice-washed jeans. Her new tan boots would complete the outfit, but Sarah had the nagging feeling that something was missing — that little touch that would make her stand out from everyone else. On an impulse, she added a long string of Indian wooden beads, and knotted a brown-and-yellow madras cloth around her waist for a belt. Perfect.

"I can't believe he's so eager to go out with you," Micki said thoughtfully later that day. They were standing in the hall after math class, their final period of the day.

"Thanks a lot," Sarah joked. She shoved her books under her arm and wondered if she should make a final check in the girls' room. Her hair always frizzed a little when it was humid, and it might be a good idea to run a brush through it.

"You know I didn't mean it that way," Micki said with an apologetic grin. "I just meant that his sudden interest is kind of . . . sudden." She stared seriously at her friend. "By the way, you look great today. And don't worry about your hair. It's perfect."

"That's good to know," Sarah told her ruefully. As usual, Micki seemed to read her mind!

"I wish I was going with you," Micki said wistfully. "But I guess that would look a little funny."

"Just a little." They stepped out in the bright sunlight and Sarah glanced at her watch. She'd be seeing Cody in just fifteen minutes. She wondered why he hadn't asked her to meet him outside school and then they could have walked over to Carmichael's together.

"Well, I just wish I was a fly on the wall," Micki said mischievously. "I bet I'd have a lot to tell."

"Maybe not as much as you'd think," Sarah said nervously.

Now that she was actually going to have her first real date with Cody, she felt a little panicky. What if it didn't go as well as she hoped? He had been madly in love with her the night before, but who knew how he'd feel today? As far as she knew, the love potion might be wearing off. In fact, what would happen if it had worn off completely? But then he wouldn't keep the date with her, would he? She frowned, wondering what she would do if he didn't show up. Or what if he showed up, but didn't act friendly? The whole situation was getting hopelessly complicated. Who would ever think that having a boy fall in love with you would make you feel so confused?

Cody was drumming his fingers on a back table at Carmichael's when Sarah approached him warily a few minutes later. He looked as terrific as ever, but the drumming fingers made her a little nervous. She had no idea if he was annoyed, impatient, or maybe even having second thoughts about seeing her.

She didn't have to wonder long, though, because the minute he spotted her, he jumped to his feet with a thousand-kilowatt smile.

"Sarah!" he cried, crushing her in a bear hug. After several moments, he drew back and looked at her tenderly. "Oh, Sarah," he said, "I can't believe you're really here."

"Well, of course I'm here," she said happily, easing herself into the chair. He was glad to see her — in fact, he was ecstatic. Some girls at the next table were watching them with interest, and Sarah recognized one of them from her French class. She could just imagine the envious looks she'd get the next day when the word got out that she had been at Carmichael's with Cody Rice.

He leaned across the table and clasped her hand, his eyes starry with love. "It's just . . . so wonderful to see you," he said. "Like a miracle."

A miracle? The waitress cleared her throat noisily just then, and Cody reluctantly pulled his eyes off her long enough to order fries and sodas for both of them.

When the waitress left, Sarah searched her

mind frantically for something to talk about. She still felt a little nervous. After all, Cody was the most terrific boy in the whole school, and he was probably used to girls who always knew what to say. She always found it hard to talk to boys she didn't know very well. She tried to remember the advice she had read in a magazine that month, and decided to talk about sports.

"That was some football practice yesterday," she said brightly. "I think Anderson is going to make a great quarterback, don't you?"

Cody gave her an incredibly sweet smile. "I never even noticed him," he said softly.

"How could you miss him?" Sarah said. "He was streaking all over the field making touch-downs." She was talking too fast, and her throat was tight with nervousness. Cody didn't seem to know or care, though, and gave her hand an affectionate squeeze. He had never taken his eyes off her, she noticed. Not from the moment she had sat down. She started to say something else when Cody kissed her hand. She had no idea what she was supposed to do, and when she glanced at the next table, she saw that the girl from her French class was watching them in amazement.

Cody gave her a dreamy look. "I wasn't

watching the game," he admitted. "I only had eyes for you."

"Oh. Uh, that's nice." He seemed to be waiting for her to say something else. "That's very sweet of you."

Sarah was groping in her mind for another subject when Cody said, "You know, I've never met anyone like you, Sarah. You're everything I've ever wanted in a girlfriend."

A girlfriend! This was the news she was waiting for! Today was going to be the start of a whole wonderful relationship with Cody.

"Do you really mean that?" she said softly.

"Of course I do." Cody's voice was low and sincere. The look in his eyes was unmistakable. "I could never find another girl like you, Sarah. Not if I looked for a hundred years. You're . . . different."

You don't know how different, Sarah thought.

She took a deep breath and started to relax. Everything was going to be all right. In fact, it was going to be perfect! Giving Cody the love potion had been the best idea she'd ever had.

He began kissing her fingers again, keeping those blue eyes focused on her the whole time, and Sarah sneaked a look at the girls at the next table. They were staring openmouthed now, but Cody seemed oblivious to them.

"When I am I going to see you again?" he murmured.

"Whenever you want," Sarah said. So much for playing hard-to-get! The sodas and french fries arrived just then, and Cody winked at her and let go of her hand.

"How does tomorrow sound? I've got a surprise for you," Cody said playfully.

Sarah reached for a french fry and stared at him. This had been a day full of surprises! "Really — what's that?" She tried to keep her voice light, but she could hardly contain her excitement.

"You're not going to believe the terrific weekend I've got planned for us."

"Why don't you tell me about it," she said huskily.

For the next few minutes, Cody rambled on happily about long walks on the beach and picnics in the park. He wanted to take her to a romantic place for dinner and dance the night away under the stars. He had a lifetime of plans for the two of them. Together forever.

All her wishes were coming true, she thought happily. It was all so wonderful, and so unbelievable, she felt like pinching herself.

But it's not a dream, she told herself. Cody Rice really is in love with me!

"How did it go with Cody?" Micki phoned to ask her that evening. It was eight-thirty, and Sarah was curled up on her bed with Bandit, trying on a new shade of nail polish she had borrowed from Nicole.

"It was . . . wonderful," she said slowly. "Better than I had ever imagined."

"Really!" Micki cried. "Well, tell me everything," she insisted. "What did he say, what did you say, and most important of all, are you going to see him again?"

Sarah paused. It would be hard to repeat the things Cody had told her. What would Micki think? She'd never understand that a perfect stranger had fallen madly in love with her. Especially a perfect stranger who happened to look like Cody!

"He's very nice. He told me a little about himself, and he said he was really glad we had met each other." She didn't like fibbing to Micki, but that wasn't stretching the truth *too* much, she decided. After all, he *had* said he was glad they had met — he had even said that Sarah was "his destiny." She decided to leave that part out, though. There was no sense in making Micki suspicious. Somehow, when the time was right, she'd tell her the whole story of Cody and the love potion.

"Well, are you going to see him again?" Micki prodded.

"Am I ever!" Sarah laughed. "If he had his way, I'd see him twenty-four hours a day."

"You're kidding!"

"No, I'm not," Sarah said seriously. "You should hear what he's got planned for this weekend. . . ." She quickly outlined the dates that Cody had set up, and when she finished, there was a long silence.

"Wow, it sounds like you two are going to be spending a lot of time together." Sarah flinched at the wistful note in Micki's voice. "Hey, you'll still have time for your old friends, won't you?" Her voice was only half-teasing.

"Of course," Sarah said warmly. "You're my best friend in the whole world, Micki. I'm never going to forget that."

They stayed on the phone for another ten minutes, and Sarah couldn't stop feeling a little guilty about deceiving Micki. Naturally Micki wouldn't understand why Cody had fallen so hard for her, because Micki didn't know about the love potion. And she wouldn't understand about the love potion, because she didn't know that Sarah was a witch.

Chapter 11

"Are you sure you're comfortable?" Cody asked solicitiously. It was noon on Saturday and Sarah and Cody were having a picnic at Harper's Landing, a small leafy park down by the river.

"I'm fine." They were sitting side by side on a blue-and-white plaid blanket with a large bag from Genardo's delicatessen between them. "But I'm starving!" she added. "I guess I worked up an appetite on that long walk." She gave him a shy smile. They had walked along the embankment hand in hand for a couple of hours, enjoying the warm day, and tossing bread crumbs to a noisy group of mallard ducks.

It was one of the most wonderful days Sarah had ever spent. She didn't know much about boys, but as far as she could tell, Cody was the perfect date; he was incredibly good-looking, he was fun to be with, and most important of all — he was crazy about her! If she had tried to invent the ideal boy, she couldn't have done a better job.

"Let's open the sandwiches," he suggested, reaching into the bag. "Take your pick, but I have to warn you," he teased, "they're all the same. Corned beef and swiss cheese on poppyseed rolls with mustard."

Sarah raised her eyebrows. "Really? But that's my favorite sandwich in the whole world. How did you know? You must be psychic."

"Afraid not," Cody told her. "I called your sister Nicole early this morning, and asked her."

"I can't believe you'd go to all that trouble," Sarah said. Impulsively, she reached over and squeezed his hand. "You've got to be the most considerate boy I've ever met."

"Nothing's too good for you, Sarah." Cody's piercing blue eyes were serious. "When you love somebody, you want to do everything for them."

When you love somebody! Sarah was speechless. Not only was she on a real date with the most terrific boy at Waterview High, but he was in love with her. If this was an example of what being a witch could achieve, she could hardly wait to experiment some more.

It was nearly sunset when Cody walked her home, and when they got to the front porch, he kissed her very lightly on the lips.

"I had a wonderful time," Sarah started to say, but he cut her off.

"It's not over yet. You didn't think I was saying good-bye, did you?"

"Well, I — " Sarah never finished what she as about to say, because he swept her into a hug, and for a few moments her face was buried against his warm flannel shirt.

Cody chuckled and released her. "It's almost six," he said, glancing at his watch. "That should give you plenty of time to get ready."

"Get ready?" Sarah was baffled.

"For dinner and dancing. Don't tell me you've forgotten." He pretended to be angry, but his eyes were full of laughter.

"Tonight?" Sarah looked at her dusty jeans in dismay.

"Of course tonight. See you in an hour," he said eagerly.

Sarah felt so dazed she could hardly pull her thoughts together. "Terrific," she finally murmured.

* * *

On Monday at school, Micki insisted on hearing every detail of her day with Cody.

"I thought the picnic was the most fantastic thing that ever happened to me, but later that night we went dancing!" They were standing in the main corridor, waiting for the first bell to ring, and were being jostled from all sides.

"We went to that new place, Duffy's — you know, the one that advertises 'dancing under the stars.' It's on top of a hill, and they set up speakers so you can dance outside on this stone patio. And they have Japanese lanterns, and dozens of tiny lights threaded in the trees. . . ."

"Wow," Micki said, impressed. "Duffy's is supposed to cost a fortune. He must have blown his allowance for the next six months."

"He probably did," Sarah admitted. She lowered her voice. "But you know what he said? He said *nothing* was too good for the girl he loves."

Micki was stunned. "He said he *loves* you? You're kidding!"

"No, it's true." The bell rang just then, cutting off their conversation, and Micki groaned. "Don't worry, I'll tell you all about it later," Sarah promised.

By midmorning, Sarah was surprised to find

that news of her new relationship with Cody had spread through her class. Tina Jordan stopped her in the hall to say that her sister had seen her dancing at Duffy's with a "fantastic-looking guy," and Heather Larson passed her a note from Cody after French class.

"He knows you and I are friends," Heather explained, her blue eyes puzzled. "And he said he had an urgent message for you." She handed her a crumpled piece of notebook paper that had been folded so many times it was the size of a matchbook. "I hope it's nothing serious," she added, peering at Sarah.

"I don't think it's anything to worry about," Sarah said. Heather stood waiting while she unwrapped the note, and looked disappointed when Sarah read it quickly and shoved it in her pocket.

"Well?" Heather said eagerly.

"It's . . . sort of personal," Sarah told her, grinning. The note had consisted of a little red heart with their initials on it, and a single sentence written on the bottom.

"Personal? Now you've really made me curious. I think I should tell you that there's a rumor going around school that you and Cody — " she stopped when she saw Sarah's delighted expression. "You don't mean that it's true? You and Cody are going out together?"

Sarah nodded. "Better than that. It looks like we're going steady."

"Doesn't it seem like things are moving awfully fast with you and Cody?" Micki asked pointedly. Sarah had invited Micki to come home with her after school that day, and they were sitting at the kitchen table, finishing off thick wedges of chocolate cake.

"What do you mean?" Sarah hedged.

"Well, gosh, Sarah, you just met him, and all of a sudden he wants to go steady."

"It's not that sudden," Sarah protested. "We've had about four dates."

"But they were all over one weekend."

"True. I guess you'd call it quality time." Sarah sipped her milk slowly, thinking how handsome Cody had looked down by the river in his faded jeans and flannel shirt. She had never been happier in her life.

"I guess I'm a little worried about you," Micki was saying seriously. "I just don't want you rushing into anything."

"Oh, Micki," Sarah said, taking her hand. "I'm not rushing into anything. I've thought this out very carefully. I. . . ." How could she begin to explain? Of course Micki was puzzled.

She didn't know why Cody was suddenly in love with her, because she didn't know Sarah was a witch.

"Just don't get in over your head," Micki said worriedly.

"I won't," Sarah promised. "I know exactly what I'm doing."

During the next few days, Sarah found out exactly what it was like to be the object of Cody Rice's adoration. It was thrilling, but it was also exhausting. She had never suspected that a love-struck Cody would expect to spend every waking moment with her, but that's exactly what he had in mind. He dashed into her homeroom to see her before the bell rang. He chased her down the hall between classes, and he left love notes stuck in her locker door. Once he even left a pale white orchid fastened to her combination lock. She had no idea what do with it, and finally pressed it between the pages of her history book as a souvenir.

The nightly phone calls were beginning to get on her mother's nerves. Cody called five or six times every evening, and Sarah finally had to tell him she could only talk to him once after dinner.

"Once after dinner?" he had moaned. "How will I get through the whole evening without you?"

For the first time, Sarah felt a flicker of annoyance. "Well, you could try studying," she suggested. She was sitting in bed, struggling with her math homework, wondering how she could possibly finish her problems by the next day.

"Studying?"

"Or watch TV, or read . . . Oh, I don't know, there must be a million things you could do," she said impatiently.

There was a long pause, and she wondered if he was angry enough to hang up on her. She heard him sigh, and then he said in a sad voice, "If I can't talk to you whenever I want to, Sarah, I'll do the next best thing. I'll write to you."

Sarah was exasperated. "You already write to me, Cody. I find your notes in my locker every day."

"But this way I can write to you more," he said eagerly. "Not just notes, but letters, long letters. . . ." She let him ramble on for a few minutes, and then she said her mother needed her in the kitchen. After she finally got him off the line, she picked up her math book and turned to Bandit, who was sprawled across her pillow.

"Bandit," she said softly, "I'm beginning to wonder what I let myself in for."

The next morning, Sarah woke up to the sound of someone hammering on the front door. "Honey, can you get that?" her mother called. "I'm not dressed."

"Neither am I," Sarah muttered, stumbling out of bed and into her robe. She brushed her dark hair out of her eyes and hurried down the hall. If this is Cody Rice . . . she thought grimly.

She threw open the front door, and someone thrust a bulky envelope in her hands. "Sarah Connell?" a man in a uniform asked.

"Yes, but — "

"Sign here." She scribbled her name on a slip of paper, and the man tipped his hat and left. Puzzled, she walked slowly into the kitchen, opening the envelope.

"Hey, what's that — instant express?" Simon asked. He was working his way through a stack of waffles. "Is it for you?"

Sarah shrugged. "I guess so, but I can't

imagine — oh, no!" she said, as she pulled out a sheaf of pale blue stationery. She recognized the handwriting immediately as Cody's. *My dearest, darling Sarah*, the letter began. She quickly flipped through the pages — there were twenty sheets of paper, with writing on both sides!

"What is it?" Simon asked, half rising out of his chair.

"It's nothing. It's a . . . mistake," she said quickly, shoving everything back into the envelope.

"A mistake?"

Sarah turned and headed back to her room. "It's a long story," she tossed over her shoulder.

When she got to school that morning, Cody was waiting by her locker.

"Did you get my letter?" he asked eagerly.

"I sure did," she told him, patting her notebook. She started to stash her books in her locker, when Cody grabbed her arm excitedly.

"I'm so glad," he said feelingly. "I just caught the night mail before the truck went out."

Sarah stared at him. "You went into the city to mail this to me?"

"At ten o'clock at night," he said, nodding vigorously. "I wanted you to think of me first thing this morning."

"You shouldn't have gone to so much trouble," Sarah said helplessly.

Cody took a step closer, and gently put his hands on her shoulders. His eyes were very blue and his white shetland sweater clung to his broad shoulders. "You know how I feel about you, Sarah. And when you love someone — "

"Nothing is too good for them," Sarah parroted. "I know, I know — you've told me before," she said, brushing away his hands. The bell rang just then, and she had the perfect excuse to push him away and flee down the hall. She threw herself in her homeroom seat and looked around nervously to make sure Cody hadn't followed her. Thank goodness, she thought. One thing was sure: Cody Rice was driving her crazy!

The final straw came that day at lunchtime. Since Cody's class schedule was different, he never had the chance to sit with her at lunch, but this particular afternoon was an exception. Sarah was with Matt Neville, waiting for Micki and Tina to go through the line, when Cody dashed over to their table.

"Here you are!" he said happily. "Guess what, my chemistry class was canceled, so we can spend a whole half hour together!" He started to pull out a chair, but stopped when he saw Matt Neville. "Who are you?" he asked bluntly.

"This is Matt Neville," Sarah explained. "We're waiting for — "

"What's he doing here?" Cody's voice was harsh.

"Cody!" Sarah gasped. "What's gotten into you?"

"I need to talk to you alone," Cody said stubbornly.

"That's fine with me," Matt said, pushing his glasses up on his nose. "I want to get some dessert anyway." He waved his hand when Sarah started to protest, and headed for the serving line.

"I can't believe you did that!" Sarah said angrily.

"I can't believe I found you sitting with another guy," Cody retorted. He sat down next to her, and put his hand on the back of her chair. His blue eyes were cold and angry.

"Another guy? Matt and I are friends," Sarah explained. "I've known him for *years* — "

"I don't want to hear about it," Cody said, cutting her off. "The point is, you and I are going steady, and that means you don't sit with anyone else. Not at lunch, not anywhere."

"But that's crazy!" Sarah protested. Out of the corner of her eye, she saw Micki and Tina watching her curiously. They were paying the cashier and would be at the table any minute. Matt was dawdling over the dessert section, probably trying to stall as long as he could.

"We *are* going steady, aren't we?" he demanded. "I asked you to, last week."

"I was thinking it over," Sarah hesitated. She had never answered his note, but now she had made up her mind. There was no way she would go steady with him.

"What's to think over?" Cody glowered and jumped to his feet as Micki plunked her tray down. "I'll talk to you later, Sarah." He crossed the cafeteria quickly and bounded up the stairs.

"Wow," Micki said softly. "What's up?"

Sarah glanced at Tina and Matt, who were approaching the table. "I'll tell you all about it after lunch," she said. Who would ever think that being adored could cause so many problems?

Chapter 12

"I never meant for it to turn out this way," Sarah moaned to Aunt Pam a couple of days later. "Cody's driving me nuts. It was a big mistake to make him fall in love with me." It was late afternoon, and Sarah was alone in the kitchen, with the phone tucked against her chin as she whipped up a batch of chocolate chip cookies.

"Well," Aunt Pam said with a throaty chuckle, "I hate to say 'I told you so,' but I told you so!"

"I know you did," Sarah agreed. "But the question is, what can I do about it now? How can I get rid of Cody Rice?"

"Exactly how much of the potion did you give him?"

Sarah frowned in thought. "Maybe a tablespoon. A *big* tablespoon. I was afraid to give him more than that — in case he tasted it in the lemonade."

"Thank goodness for that," Aunt Pam said feelingly. Sarah could hear the rustle of pages, and she wrapped her fingers nervously around the phone cord. There was a long pause, and then Aunt Pam said cheerfully, "I think you can relax now. According to my calculations, the spell will wear off in a few more days."

"It will?"

"You can count on it. So if you can just hold out a little longer, Cody will forget all about you. He won't have any memory of having been in love with you, and things will be back to normal. In other words, he won't even know you're alive."

"Oh, Aunt Pam," Sarah said in a rush of emotion, "you don't know how glad I am to hear that!" She did a little dance step, nearly tripping herself on the phone cord.

"Before you get too carried away, we need to talk about a few things. For example. . . ." Aunt Pam felt compelled to give Sarah another lecture then, and Sarah did her best to sound remorseful. She was glad that Aunt Pam couldn't see her face, though, because she was grinning from ear to ear. She was off the hook!

In just a few days, she'd be rid of Cody forever.

Sarah did her best to avoid Cody Rice for the next couple of days, even though he managed to wedge several more love notes in her locker door.

A more serious problem faced her one morning in history class: She had been so caught up worrying about Cody, she completely forgot to study for a test on the Civil War!

When Ms. Hines said the dreaded words, "Take out a sheet of paper," Sarah was stunned.

"The most important part of the test is the essay question," Ms. Hines said. "But I've also included some multiple choice and fill-in-the-blanks. . . ." She started handing out thick stacks of mimeographed sheets. "The test covers everything in the textbook, and everything we talked about in class," she added grimly.

"Great," Sarah muttered softly. She had never been so totally unprepared for a test in her life. She had been daydreaming in class lately — which she knew was a big mistake — and to make matters worse, she was several chapters behind in her reading.

She looked at the questions and drew a blank. Names and places seemed to jump off the page at her — Appomattox, Vicksburg, abolition, and something called the Missouri Compromise. What in the world was that? she wondered. And there were dozens of dates and battles and famous generals, too. She squeezed her eyes shut and tried to remember something — *anything* — about the Civil War. It was hopeless! Well, almost. The only thing she could recall about General Lee was that his horse was named Traveller and that the two of them were buried side by side in Virginia. Somehow she didn't think that was the kind of question that Ms. Hines would bother asking.

What could she do? She looked around the classroom, and everyone else was hard at work on the test. The room was completely still except for the sound of scratching pens, and of course, the clock, which was mercilessly ticking away the minutes. She caught Ms. Hines's eye, and looked away quickly. The last thing she wanted to do was let the teacher know that anything was wrong. She'd have to figure this one out for herself.

But how? Cheating was out of the question. She had never cheated in her life and wasn't going to start now. Just the idea of copying someone's paper was so sleazy that — she wouldn't *have* to cheat. She could use magic! After all, what was the use of being a witch if you couldn't use it to get out of tight spots? She knew that Aunt Pam would howl if she found out, but this was no time to worry about minor details. She glanced at the clock again, rubbing her damp palms on her skirt. She had already wasted ten minutes. This was an emergency!

The first thing was to tackle the multiple choice questions. It was much easier than Sarah had imagined. She moved her pencil slowly down the page, and after squeezing her eyes and making a wish, the pencil stopped at the right answer. At least, Sarah assumed it was the right answer. Halfway through the test, she sneezed, and the pencil jumped around a little, but she just closed her eyes again and got it back on track.

She watched, fascinated, as the pencil traveled down the page. Amazing! She finished the questions quickly, but pretended to struggle with a few of them, in case Ms. Hines was watching her with her eagle eyes.

When fifteen minutes had gone by, Sarah took a deep breath and decided to tackle the essay question. She had no idea how to begin, but she was sure that her magic powers would guide her.

> *Discuss the sociological, political, and economic issues that led to the Civil War, and be sure to include both the Wilmot Proviso and the Compromise of 1850 in your answer. Be precise, using all relevant data.*

Sarah read the question twice and smiled. *Be precise!* Ms. Hines really knew how to twist the knife.

She squeezed her eyes shut again, thinking. This was going to be a lot tougher than the multiple choice, because as Ms. Hines always said, essay questions are very personal. They should come out of your own opinions, and, of course, your own reading on the subject.

Wait a minute, Sarah thought. There must be some way a witch could do some reading right now. All she needed to do was get to the library. But how? Could she actually travel through space? Could she transport herself from one room to another, just by wishing it? It was worth a try. She concentrated as hard as she could. When she opened her eyes, she was thrilled to find that it had worked. She was in the library! She raced over to the reference section and selected one of the big dog-eared encyclopedia volumes.

She hoisted the book onto the table and thumbed through it until she found the section on the Civil War. Suddenly a section caught her eye: *The Issues That Led to the War*. Perfect. That was exactly what she wanted. She scanned the page, absorbing every word. Finally, she decided she had read enough. She squeezed her eyes shut, opened them cautiously, and she was back in history class! Amazingly, she could still *see* the encyclopedia page. It was just like the words were printed on her brain. All she had to do was copy them.

When the bell rang, Sarah dropped her paper quickly on the desk, trying not to look at Ms. Hines. Micki finished at the same time, and the two of them fell into step in the hall.

"What did you think about it?" Micki whispered nervously. "The pits, right?"

"Oh, it wasn't too bad," Sarah said hesitantly. Once again, she found herself lying to Micki. If only she could blurt out the truth!

"Not too *bad*?" Micki wailed. "I wish I had your confidence. I think my A average just went right down the drain. And the essay — that was the worst!"

A moment later, they were joined by Tina

Jordan, and a shell-shocked Heather Larson. "Wow," Heather said softly. "I couldn't even *understand* the essay question, much less answer it. How did you do, Sarah?"

On the spot again, Sarah thought. "Oh, I think the essay question was pretty fair," she said vaguely.

"You do?" Three pairs of eyes turned to her in amazement.

Sarah wondered if it was possible for a witch to keep friends.

"I just know I blew it," Heather said in a little voice. "I answered the whole thing in half a page."

"I didn't do much better," Tina admitted. "And as far as the Missouri Compromise went — forget it!"

Sarah found herself tuning out while the four of them ambled down the hall, still discussing the test. She felt guilty about the way she had aced the test — but what else could she do under the circumstances? Of course, it would have been better if she had studied like everyone else, and she was sure Aunt Pam would raise the roof if she found out.

Everyone was heading over to Carmichael's, but Sarah decided to go home and do some research. She had Aunt Pam's *Spells and Potions* book hidden under her bed, and she wanted to take another look at it. The spell she had put on Cody Rice had been a disaster, but you couldn't really blame the potion, she decided. Who could have predicted that he would turn out to be so boring? And it had worked, all right. He *was* madly in love with her.

She was skipping up the steps to her front porch, when she suddenly stopped. Cody Rice was sitting on her porch swing! She instinctively started to back down the steps, but it was too late. He had seen her, and had already jumped out of the swing, with a dumb, puppy-like look of devotion on his face.

"Sarah!" he gasped, running to her. She shuddered and flattened herself against a pillar. She knew what was coming. First a crushing embrace, and then several minutes of adoring stares. She didn't think she could take it!

"Hi, Cody," she said, putting her books up like a shield.

Nothing fazed Cody. He clasped her to him, books and all, nearly lifting her off her feet in his enthusiasm. "This is the moment I've been waiting for!" he said feelingly.

"What are you doing here?" Sarah said ungraciously. She managed to separate herself from Cody, and began edging toward the front door. Maybe if she could distract him for a moment, she could make a run for it.

"Well, I'm here to see you, of course," he said, laughing. He threw his arms up in a dramatic gesture. "Where else should I be? What else should I be doing?"

Actually, Sarah could think of a million other things he could be doing, but didn't have the nerve to say so. The trick with Cody was going to be to find out what he wanted, and then get rid of him — fast.

"You wouldn't believe the plans I've got for this weekend," he said playfully.

"I'm sure I would," Sarah muttered, gauging the distance to the door. Cody must have read her mind, because he suddenly moved, cutting off her escape route.

"Oh, no, you can't," he teased.

"Oh, yes, I can," Sarah said. This game could go on forever, unless she took firm action now!

"Tell me," he said, surprising her, "what's your favorite color?"

Was it a trick question, she wondered? "My favorite color?" she said. "Well, I like yellow, I guess."

"Then yellow it will be!" Cody said, clapping his hands together excitedly.

"Yellow *what* will be?" Sarah asked suspiciously.

"Yellow flowers, dozens of them." He smiled, waiting for her to say something.

"You're sending me flowers?"

He nodded, and tried to take her hands in his, but she was too fast for him. "Unless you'd rather have something else. Let's see, what else is yellow?" He looked away for a split second, and Sarah saw her chance.

"Oops, I hear the phone," she cried. "I've got to go in now." Before he could react, she darted past him and bolted through the front door. As she slammed it shut, she heard him say softly, "No, it has to be flowers. Only flowers will do. . . ."

Sarah double-locked the door, and stood panting in the hall for a moment. Then she turned to see Simon staring curiously at her. "Don't open that door!" she ordered. "Not under any circumstances." She ignored his amazed look and ran upstairs. She didn't think she could wait any longer for the love potion to wear off. Maybe she should check the book for an antidote!

Chapter 13

"Do you want the good news or the bad news?" Ms. Hines asked the next day in history class. She stood at the front of the room, clutching a pile of mimeographed sheets, while the class fidgeted nervously. Except for Sarah, of course. She *knew* Ms. Hines was holding the history tests, and she could hardly wait to see her grade. It would be an A, of course, but maybe Ms. Hines had added some personal comments, like "excellent work" or "top-rate."

For the moment she was safe. She was sure Ms. Hines would never know how she had aced the test. Ms. Hines's raspy voice cut into her thoughts, and Sarah sat up a little straighter in her seat. She didn't want to miss a word.

"Well, I'll give you the bad news first. Most

of you got below a C on this test." Ms. Hines paused, waiting for the words to sink in. Predictably, a groan went up from the class. "There were exceptions, of course, and one of them is sitting right in front of me." She smiled warmly at Sarah, and continued. "Not only did Sarah Connell answer all the multiple choice questions correctly, but she did an outstanding job on the essay question."

All eyes turned to Sarah, and Allison Rogers flashed her a look of sizzling hatred. Sarah could feel her face getting hot. It was nice to get an A, but why did Ms. Hines have to single her out like this? Everyone would think she was a nerd!

Unfortunately there was more to come. "I'm so impressed with Sarah's understanding of the Civil War, that I'd like her to come up here and give a brief oral report."

Sarah lurched forward in her seat, as if someone had plunged a knife in her back. "A what?" she gasped.

"An oral report," Ms. Hines said cheerfully. "Sarah, you can take the floor now."

"I . . . I . . . ."

"Now Sarah, this is no time to be shy." Ms. Hines adjusted her glasses on her nose, her expression mildly reproachful. "The rest of the class can benefit from your research."

"My research," Sarah repeated dully. Mechanically, she stumbled to the front of the room. It was almost as if she were a puppet and someone else were pulling the strings. Her mind was reeling. What would she say? She clasped her hands together and turned to Ms. Hines, who nodded reassuringly.

"You may begin," the teacher said firmly.

"I'm not sure I understand," Sarah mumbled, stalling for time.

Ms. Hines shook her head impatiently. "Just tell the class what you told me on paper, Sarah. Discuss the issues that led to the Civil War."

The issues that led to the Civil War. Suddenly something clicked in Sarah's memory, and without even meaning to, she began reciting the encyclopedia section. Word for word!

"Although one may argue that the origins of the war can be traced to our early history, there is no doubt that earlier events sparked the conflict. Among the causes were the differences in the economies of the North and South. The plantations of the South functioned with the use of slave labor. While the industrialized North did not use slaves and did not own slaves." Her voice was flat and expressionless, like a bad recording. Her hands tightened. Panic flooded through her. She couldn't stop talking! Something was very, very wrong!

She saw the startled look on Ms. Hines's face, and heard someone in the front row start to laugh, but still the voice — *her* voice — rattled on. "When the nation expanded westward, the problem became whether the new states should allow slavery or not. The Missouri Compromise in 1820. . . ."

She was racing through the paragraphs, like a tape recorder thrown on fast-forward. Names and dates flew by in a blur, and she couldn't even stop to catch her breath.

Ms. Hines had half risen from her seat, and her face was like a thundercloud. Sarah clenched her lips together very tightly, but nothing helped. She was doomed to repeat the whole encyclopedia passage word for word!

"Sarah," Ms. Hines said warningly, "if this is a joke, it's not very funny."

I don't think it's funny, either! Sarah pleaded silently. Her voice blitzed the room like a machine gun. She couldn't stop it! She had never felt so helpless, nor so idiotic in her life. She stared at Micki, whose mouth had dropped open in surprise, but the words continued to tumble out. "The slavery issue was divided sectionally, because the rich agricultural lands. . . ."

"That's enough!" Ms. Hines said in a voice that could cut glass. "That's *quite* enough, Sarah," she added forcefully. She thumped her fist on the desk. That jolted Sarah back to the real world. Back to her normal voice.

"I'm sorry," she said in a whispery voice. She felt almost faint with relief. At least it was over.

"Just take your seat, Sarah," Ms. Hines snapped. She waited until Sarah had slunk back to her desk before saying, "That was a brilliant display. Of *memory* work," she added sarcastically. "All you've shown me is that you have a photographic memory. You had no idea in the world what you were saying, did you?"

Mortified, Sarah bit her lip and shook her head. She shaded her eyes with her hand, wondering if she'd ever live this moment down.

She could feel Ms. Hines's eyes on her, and she slowly looked up. The teacher's voice was stern. "Knowledge isn't memorization, Sarah. It's understanding. There's a big difference between the two. Do you know what I'm talking about?"

Sarah nodded, dangerously close to tears.

"If I had wanted a . . . magic act, I would have brought a talking dog to class," Ms. Hines went on scathingly. Sarah recognized a high-pitched giggle from the second row. Allison Rogers. "You can save your . . . tricks . . . for drama class, Sarah. I expected better from you."

When the bell rang half an hour later, Sarah wanted to escape from the classroom as quickly as possible. Micki, her brown eyes warm with sympathy, touched her arm lightly, and together they bolted for the door.

They had barely stepped into the hall when Allison's grating voice caught up with them. "Hey, Sarah!" she yelled. "Nice going!" Sarah turned in time to see Allison make an "okay" sign to her, and then double up with laughter.

"Ignore her," Micki advised through gritted teeth.

"A talking dog act!" another voice giggled. "Who would ever think Ms. Hines was such a comedian."

"C'mon," Micki said urgently. She grabbed Sarah's sleeve and half-dragged her down the hall. Sarah was moving in a daze. How could being a witch have let her down like that! *Something* had gone wrong.

Still guiding Sarah, Micki pushed open the heavy double doors that led outside to the playing field. It was a bright October day, and Sarah flinched as the sunlight hit her eyes.

"Where are we going?" she protested. At the moment, all she wanted to do was find a hole and crawl in it.

"I told Tina Jordan we'd get together at the track meet today. You didn't forget, did you? We're playing Tannersville." She glanced at her watch and said meaningfully, "It doesn't start for another half hour, so that gives us plenty of time to talk." She gestured to the faded blue bleachers that ringed the field. "Let's find a spot in the shade and get comfortable."

"I don't know . . ." Sarah said. The last thing she wanted to do was talk. She knew that Micki was going to question her, and she had no answers!

"C'mon, Sarah," Micki was saying urgently. She had climbed the bleachers and was waiting for Sarah to join her.

"Okay," Micki said the minute Sarah was settled, "now what was that all about?"

Sarah hesitated. "I . . . can't explain it," Sarah said finally. At least that part is true! she thought.

"But Sarah," Micki protested, "why did you go on like that in class? Ms. Hines is really going to have it in for you now. She thinks you were trying to be funny or something."

"Believe me, if I could have stopped, I would have," Sarah said feelingly. "The words just kept pouring out."

Micki frowned, deep in thought. "But how did you know all those names and dates? You sounded just like the encyclopedia."

Sarah nodded unhappily. "I guess I was concentrating so hard, trying to remember what I read . . . that I repeated the section, word for word. I could see the page in my mind."

"Actually, it was pretty impressive," Micki said, with a sudden smile. "I'm beginning to think you must have a photographic memory."

"Something like that," Sarah said eagerly. She hoped Micki would be satisfied with this explanation for now. She wasn't ready to tell Micki the truth just yet.

At that moment, Tina Jordan, Heather Larson, Erin Chambers, and Matt Neville crowded in next to them, putting an end to their private conversation. Sarah breathed a sigh of relief. She had been given a reprieve, but she knew she wasn't off the hook. She knew how persistent Micki could be.

"Hi, Kirk!" Sarah's ears perked up as Matt Neville yelled a greeting to Waterview's star runner. At the same moment, Micki nudged her sharply in the ribs.

"Look, that's Kirk Tanner," Micki hissed. "Do something!"

Sarah smiled. "What should I do? Throw myself off the bleachers to attract his attention?"

Micki said, "Oh, right. You have Cody now."

Sarah made a face. "No, Cody Rice is definitely history," she said firmly. "He just doesn't know it yet." She watched as Kirk Tanner made his way slowly across the field toward them. He really *was* good-looking, she decided, with sandy hair, broad shoulders, and a warm smile. It's funny to think that she had let Cody Rice take her attention away from Kirk. Just a few weeks before, she had thought Kirk Tanner was the most exciting boy in the whole world.

Kirk had reached the bleachers then, and Heather Larson was looking up at him adoringly. "I *love* the editorial you wrote," she said in her little-girl voice. "And I hope you come in first today."

"Thanks," Kirk said, flashing that million-dollar grin. "Tannersville's good," he said rue-

fully. "I'm going to need all the help I can get."
He was wearing a light gray track suit that
matched his eyes, and he stretched his long
arms out to the sides, and then crossed them
over his chest. "I never should have agreed to
edit the paper *and* be on the track team." He
laughed. "Only a magician could pull it off."

He started talking to Matt Neville then
about Waterview's chances, but Sarah could
still his words ringing in her ears. *A magician!*
Could she give him the magic he needed to win?
Did she dare? She knew she was taking a terrible chance. Her previous experiences with
magic had been total disasters! Maybe she'd
only make things worse. She frowned and tried
to remember what she had read about good-
luck charms in Aunt Pam's book. She vaguely
remembered that anything could be used as a
good-luck charm, as long as a witch blew on it
three times and mumbled the right phrase.

Sarah checked to make sure no one was
watching her, and then rummaged in her poc-
ketbook. There must be *something* she could
give Kirk that would help him win the race!
She nearly cried in despair when all she came
up with was three facial tissues, some pennies,
and a plastic comb. Then she spotted a white

pigeon's feather lying on the ground, just a few feet away. She bent over to get it and, pretending to cough, blew on it three times. She said the magic words she remembered as fast as she could — Kirk was already starting to move away!

"Kirk!" she said desperately. "Take this — for luck. There's no time to explain."

She handed him the feather, and tried to look reassuring. "It's . . . a lucky feather," she told him. "Just carry it with you, and you'll come in first place."

Kirk looked baffled, but nodded his thanks, and pocketed the feather. He moved off as the track coach called everyone over to the sidelines, and Micki turned to Sarah in amazement. "You're just *full* of surprises today, aren't you?"

When Sarah returned to the bleachers, Micki stared at her curiously. Luckily her friends were cheering so loudly, there was no chance for Micki to ask any more questions. Waterview was doing much better than anyone had expected.

The real test would be Kirk Tanner, Sarah thought nervously. He was running the hundred-yard dash, and according to Matt, he was up against one of Tannersville's best athletes.

"See number sixty-six?" Matt yelled to Sarah. "His nickname's 'Lightning.' He won the all-state competition last year."

"I'll bet Kirk can outrun him," Heather said loyally.

I'll bet he can, too! Sarah said silently. Wouldn't everyone be surprised if they knew Kirk was *guaranteed* to win — the magic feather would put him ahead of the pack.

When the gun went off for Kirk's event, Sarah was tense with excitement. She covered her eyes for most of the race, and when she opened them, Kirk and number sixty-six were neck and neck! She could see that Kirk was trying as hard as he could. His face was pale with exhaustion, and the muscles in his neck were standing out in sharp ridges.

"I can't take this," she moaned to Micki and promptly covered her eyes again.

A few seconds later, she heard a huge whoop go up from her section, and Micki grabbed her and starting jumping up and down. "He won! He did it!" Micki gasped.

Sarah opened her eyes to see a tired-looking

Kirk pushing his way to the judge's stand to accept his award. "*We* did it," she said softly.

"What did you say?" Micki looked puzzled.

Sarah grinned. "Nothing. It's . . . kind of a long story."

"C'mon," Micki said. "We've got fifteen minutes before the next event. How about grabbing a soft drink?"

Sarah nodded. "Sounds good to me." Her blouse was sticking to her, and her face was flushed with excitement. She could hardly wait to congratulate Kirk. What would he say to her? Would he know that it was the feather that pushed him over the finish line?

When they saw him on the sidelines a few minutes later, he was surrounded by his friends. When Micki went to the concession stand, Sarah wandered over to him, trying to look casual.

"You were great," she said, standing close to him.

"Thanks." He grinned. "I didn't think I'd make it there for a minute, but I suddenly got my second wind, right near the end."

"You were certainly flying over the finish line." She waited for him to mention the feather.

Kirk sipped some lemonade thoughtfully and shook his head. "It was amazing. I felt like someone was actually *pushing* me over the line."

"You did?" Sarah asked breathlessly. "Uh, Kirk, I know this sounds silly, but do you think I could have my feather back? I know it looks like an *ordinary* feather, but it really is . . . lucky." As you well know! she longed to add.

"Oh, your feather!" Kirk hit his head in mock dismay. "Gosh, I'm sorry. It blew away right before the race started. I bent down to tie my shoe and it slipped out of my pocket." He grinned sheepishly. "Maybe I could get you another one. . . ."

"That's okay," Sarah said quickly. "It wasn't important — really." If he hadn't had the feather, then he'd won on his own. So much for her magic powers. She was heading back to the concession stand when a voice made her turn.

"Sarah," Kirk said. "That was very nice of you." His gray eyes crinkled when he smiled, and he looked very handsome standing in the dusty field.

"Anytime," Sarah said lightly. "See you around."

He's really cute, Sarah thought. Maybe I

should have tried the love potion on him. It isn't really too late to. . . .

SARAH! A loud voice said in her head. Don't you ever learn?

Get off my back, Sarah said silently to the voice. *I'm just an apprentice.*

Chapter 14

"Oh dear," Aunt Pam said thoughtfully. It was nearly six-thirty in the evening, and the warm glow from the streetlights filtered inside her cheery apartment. She sighed and settled herself more comfortably on a giant blue-and-white throw pillow on the floor. Grumble darted into her lap and she stroked his fur absently for a minute, watching her niece's expression. "Things haven't been going too well for you, have they?"

"The past few days have been a total disaster," Sarah answered feelingly. She had managed to escape from Micki right after the track meet, and for the past half hour, she'd been pouring her heart out to her aunt. She hadn't held anything back, and Aunt Pam had been warm and sympathetic. "It's all been my own stupid fault," Sarah added, remembering the awful incident in history class. "I rushed into everything without thinking, and — "

"And things got out of hand," Aunt Pam finished for her. "Well, don't be too hard on yourself," she said in a softer voice. "I suppose the temptation to try out your new powers was too much to resist . . . but I did try to warn you, you know."

"I know you did, and believe me, you were absolutely right," Sarah said. "If I ever needed to be convinced, this past week has really done it." She made a face, remembering how the spell on Cody Rice had backfired. Well, not backfired exactly — it had worked, all right. Except now she didn't *want* Cody Rice!

"It must have been disappointing to get something you wished so hard for . . . and then find out it wasn't right for you after all," Aunt Pam said wisely, her golden eyes shining.

"Did you just read my mind?" Sarah said, startled.

Aunt Pam shrugged. "A lucky guess."

The buzzer on the microwave sounded just then, and Aunt Pam scrambled to her feet. "Stay for dinner," she urged. "We have a lot to talk about."

Sarah hesitated. "Mother will be wondering where I am."

"No, she won't," Aunt Pam said, reaching for some stoneware bowls. "She knows you're over here."

"She does?" Sarah's eyebrows shot up in surprise. "Is she psychic, *too*?"

Aunt Pam giggled and stirred a huge pot of soup. "I hate to disillusion you, but I called her a few minutes ago. When you were setting up the chairs on the balcony for me."

"Oh. Then I'd love to stay." Sarah looked fondly at Aunt Pam, and started to smile. Aunt Pam was amazing. She always managed to find humor and hope in every situation. Maybe there was a solution to everything after all.

"The way I see it," Aunt Pam said a few minutes later, "no real harm has been done yet. Pulling that stunt in history class was a big mistake, of course. Your magic powers must never be used to accomplish anything dishonest, like coming up with the right answers on a test, or doing your homework for you." They were having dinner outside, on the tiny balcony off the living room, and the soft night air was alive with the sound of crickets.

"No, I see that now," Sarah said meekly.

"I'll never do that again, Aunt Pam."

"I should hope not." Aunt Pam's voice was stern. "You're going to have to regain the trust of your teacher, you know. If I were you, I'd work extra hard in history for the rest of the semester. And that means no magic, no tricks. You certainly don't want a repeat peformance in front of the class."

"I couldn't take it." Sarah shuddered and reached for a piece of sourdough bread. "The funny thing is, I've always done well in history. If I had just studied like I usually do, I would have done well on the test."

"Of course," Aunt Pam said. "That's just the point. Now," she added briskly, "tell me what's going on with Cody Rice. Still madly in love, is he?"

Sarah grinned. "Would you believe two dozen yellow flowers — all on the same day?"

Sarah felt so much better after talking to Aunt Pam, she practically skipped all the way home. She had promised to return the *Spells and Potions* book, and had agreed not to try any more experiments without her aunt's approval. In return, her aunt had offered to teach her everything she needed to know about being a witch — one step at a time — and Sarah's spirits had soared.

"Of course you'll make mistakes from time to time," Aunt Pam had warned her, "but it's all part of the learning process."

It was nearly eight o'clock when Sarah got back home, and she was surprised to see Micki sitting at the kitchen table.

"Hi, Micki," Sarah said cautiously. "What a great surprise."

"Hi, yourself," Micki answered. She exchanged a look with Nicole, who yawned and wandered into the den.

What's going on? Sarah wondered. It was almost like Nicole was leaving them alone on purpose.

"I'm sorry you had to rush right home after the track meet," Micki said pointedly. "We could have talked. You're running away a lot lately."

"Yes," Sarah said without thinking. "It's a shame but I — " She stopped, flustered. Micki must *know* she hadn't gone straight home. "I . . . had things to do," she finished lamely.

Micki's face hardened. "I called you." She waited. "Your mother said you had gone to your aunt's."

"Oh, that," Sarah ran a hand through her tousled hair and wondered how she was going to get out of this. "It was nothing, really." She hated to lie to Micki, who was looking more suspicious by the minute! She tried to think of a plausible story, but couldn't.

"You don't have to tell me *everything* you do," Micki said stiffly. "I'm not trying to pry into your life. We each have a right to privacy. It's just that I thought since we're best friends. . . ." She kept her face carefully turned toward the window, staring out at the darkened backyard, and Sarah knew that Micki's feelings were hurt.

"Listen, Micki," she blurted out, "I *have* been keeping something from you. Something important."

"You have?"

"Yes, but I want to get it all out in the open. That's why — "

Simon wandered in the kitchen just then, and Sarah moaned. "What timing," she said lightly, and motioned for Micki to follow her to her room. She stopped to grab two cans of soda from the refrigerator and scooped a giant bowl of popcorn off the table.

"Hey — " Simon started to protest, but she cut him off.

"Forget it, Simon," she said firmly. "We need this more than you do."

Once they were safely inside her bedroom, Sarah flopped onto the center of the bed, and drew her knees up to her chin. Micki's brown eyes were puzzled as she eased herself down in a cross-legged position, tucking a pillow behind her. Sarah carefully put the bowl of popcorn between them, and popped the tabs on the soft drinks.

"Well," Micki said a little nervously, "this should be interesting."

Sarah gave a short laugh. "More interesting than you can imagine," she said wryly. "We've had some pretty wild discussions in the past, Micki, but believe me, *nothing* could prepare you for this one."

"Hmmm, I wouldn't be too sure about that. What about the time you decided you wanted to get out of that blind date with Susan Harper's cousin? You *begged* me to think of a good excuse for you, and we finally decided to pretend you had a broken leg." Micki laughed. "I can't believe we cut the bed sheets up into strips and and glued them on your leg."

"My mother couldn't believe it either . . . they were brand-new sheets. And if you remember, she made me pay for them." She waited for Micki to stop laughing. "Micki, we really need to talk. . . ."

"Wait a minute," Micki pleaded, still giggling. "Remember the time I tried to teach you ballet so you could audition for *Babes in Toyland?* We stayed up half the night practicing — boy, were you awful!"

"I remember," Sarah said tightly.

"And the next day . . ." Micki gasped, trying to catch her breath, "when Mrs. O'Donnell asked where you had studied ballet, you told her, 'Paris.' " Micki howled and tumbled backward on the bed, nearly upsetting the popcorn. "Paris — what in the world were you thinking of?"

"I was only six years old," Sarah reminded her. She took a deep breath, and fingered the stitching on her patchwork quilt. "This is very different, Micki," she said quietly.

Something in her solemn tone made Micki straighten up and look interested. "Different? It sounds . . . serious."

"It is," Sarah said. "It's different, and exciting, and confusing . . . and probably a thousand other things I haven't thought of yet."

Micki rolled her eyes. "Are you going to tell me what it is, or am I going to have to guess?"

Sarah gave her a searching look and then blurted out, "Micki, I'm a witch."

There was no reaction. Micki continued to stare at her, her brown eyes twinkling with laughter, her lips quivering in a smile. She looked like she was going to burst into another fit of giggles any minute.

"And?" Micki said finally.

"And?" Sarah was puzzled.

"And what's the punchline?" Micki demanded.

"There isn't any punchline. It's the truth."

Micki took a giant swallow of soda and put the can down very carefully on the nightstand. "You shouldn't kid about things like that," she said laughing again. "For a minute, you really had me going."

"I'm not kidding," Sarah said, getting a little annoyed. "It's the *truth*."

Sarah stared at Micki for a long moment, and the room seemed very still. It was Micki who broke the silence. "You're not . . . putting me on?"

Sarah shook her head. "I'm Sarah Connell . . . teen witch."

"A witch . . . as in broomsticks and black cats, and . . ." Micki faltered.

"I don't *have* a broomstick," Sarah said defensively. She licked her lips, wondering where to begin. "Look, Micki, just hear me out."

Sarah talked for the next fifteen minutes, and told Micki everything. Micki listened carefully, and when Sarah was finally finished, she sat very still, staring at her hands.

"Well, that's it," Sarah said. Now that the truth was out, she was beginning to feel a little worried. Maybe Micki would think she was crazy. Maybe she had lost her best friend. Maybe she had just made the biggest mistake of her life.

Suddenly Micki reached across and hugged Sarah fiercely. "I'm glad you told me. It shows how much you trust me."

"Then you believe me?" Sarah asked gratefully.

"It's *hard* to believe! But if you say it's true, then I guess I have to try to believe you."

Sarah felt a lump start to rise in her throat. *"You guess? Try to?"*

"Well, Sarah, be reasonable. It isn't every day your best friend tells you she's a . . . witch. Give me a break!"

"Don't you have any questions?" Sarah asked. "I'll be glad to answer them."

"Not yet," Micki said. "Later, but right now,

I wouldn't know where to start. It's a lot to take in, all at once." She looked at Sarah. "I knew something was going on, but I never thought it was anything like *this*. A witch, eh?"

"An apprentice, Aunt Pam says. I've got a lot to learn. You see what a disaster I've made of a few things already."

They were silent for a minute, and then Micki asked, "Who else knows? Besides Aunt Pam, I mean."

"That's it," Sarah told her. "Just the three of us."

"Your mother?" Micki said questioningly.

"Not yet." Sarah hesitated. "Someday, but I'll have to think that one over for a long time. She'll freak out."

"So what comes next?" Micki asked.

"I guess my life will go on as usual, except it will have this . . . new, magical dimension to it. Anyway, tomorrow is just another school day."

Walking down the corridor in school the next afternoon, Sarah looked at everyone and thought, If they knew. What a *star* I'd be. Suddenly, coming straight toward her was Cody Rice. Sarah's first instinct was to run to the girls' room and hide. That was one place Cody wouldn't follow her. She didn't *think* he would, anyway.

But then Sarah looked at Cody again. His arm was around a girl. He was staring down at her, totally engrossed in what she was saying. When he looked up and saw Sarah, he just waved and said, "Hi," and kept walking with the girl.

He doesn't remember he was in love with me, Sarah thought. Aunt Pam had said the spell would only last a week. But Sarah thought irritably, you'd think he'd remember *something* about me. How forgettable can a girl get? She turned and watched him disappearing around a corner. Well, you know you don't want him, so just *learn* from this!

At the end of the day, Micki and Sarah walked home from school together, as they always did.

"He doesn't even remember he had this wild love for me," Sarah said.

"Who?" Micki asked.

"Who?" Sarah repeated. "Cody, of course. I passed him in the hall. He was hanging all over some girl and all he said to me, blankly at that, was 'Hi.' "

"I thought you *wanted* to get rid of him," Micki said.

"I did. I do. But that is *really* rid. Like it never happened."

"Well, the spell wore off," Micki said. "And to him it never did happen."

"Yeah." Sarah sighed.

Micki looked thoughtful for a moment and then asked, "Just answer one question. You can't read minds, can you?"

"No," Sarah said, startled. "At least, I'm pretty sure I can't."

"Good! Because now that that's settled, I'm suddenly starving. What do you say we hit Carmichael's for a pizza?"

"That's fine with me," Sarah said, puzzled. "But what does going out for pizza have to do with reading minds?"

Micki looked sheepish. "There's just one problem. You see, I'm broke, and — "

"And you want me to pay for you?"

"Unless — unless you can whip up a pizza," Micki said quickly. "Is that within your powers?"

Sarah hesitated. "I don't think so," she said slowly. "I think what happened in the cafeteria was something different. I'll have to ask Aunt Pam when I see her."

"But in the meantime. . . ."

"In the meantime, I'll treat you to a pizza at Carmichael's." She put an arm around her friend. "And *then* I'll turn you into a toad," she said sweetly.

"What?"

"Relax, Micki, I'm just kidding." Grinning from ear to ear, she turned in the direction of Carmichael's. "I promise not to use my powers on you — unless you want me to."

"I'm positive I won't," Micki said, making a face.

"Oh, don't be too sure about that," Sarah told her. "It comes in pretty handy sometimes. In fact, I could. . . ." She paused, thinking. Why not use her powers to conjure up a wonderful surprise for Micki? She wasn't sure what it should be, but it would have to be fantastic, unique, and something that Micki had always wished for. It would take some thought, but she was sure she could come up with the perfect thing.

"You could *what*?" Micki was looking at her suspiciously.

"Nothing," Sarah's dark eyes were twinkling. "Just an idea," she said gaily. "Nothing for you to worry about."

The expression on Sarah's face made Micki

uneasy. "You know what they say," she warned Sarah. "Be careful what you wish for — you might get it."

"Relax, Micki," Sarah said. "I'm getting the hang of this. It's going to be *fun*, out of sight, a blast! You'll see!"

What happens when Sarah's most outrageous wish comes true? Read Teen Witch #2, *BE CAREFUL WHAT YOU WISH FOR.*

Enter the Great

TEEN™ Witch

500 Winners!

Giveaway!

Bewitching New Series!

YOU can win a FREE bewitching key chain containing **glow-in-the-dark** heart-shaped crystals. This 4-inch clear acrylic key chain has a split ring at one end—use it for your keys…or clip it anywhere and watch it **glow!**

It's easy to enter the Teen Witch Giveaway! Just complete the coupon below and return by February 28, 1989.

Watch for *Be Careful What You Wish For #2*, coming in December wherever you buy books!

Fill in your name, age, and address below and mail coupon to: TEEN WITCH GIVEAWAY, Scholastic Inc., Dept. TW, 730 Broadway, New York, NY 10003.

Name _____ Age _____

Street _____

City, State, Zip _____

TW588